THEIRS TO ETERNITY

Davina lay back. She thought she would stay awake all night, but before long she began to drift into sleep.

She therefore did not notice the slow and careful opening of the door to her chamber, nor notice the lamp she thought was extinguished flickering in the room beyond. She did not notice the man who approached her bed nor the satisfaction that crossed his features when he saw that she slept.

She slumbered as he returned to the adjoining room, slumbered as he tilted the lamp until the oil streamed out across the carpet. She slumbered as the burning wick was lowered to meet the dark and viscous liquid.

A whoosh of flame rose in an instant, sending out tongues of fire to lap at curtains, carpets and sofas. Soon a thick, enveloping smoke, having filled Davina's sitting room, began to seep insidiously beneath her bedroom door.

Its black and oily tentacles seemed to feel their way through the air, seeking a victim, any victim, to wrap in their deadly, choking embrace.

The Barbara Cartland Pink Collection

Titles in this series

THEIRS TO ETERNITY

BARBARA CARTLAND

Barbaracartland.com Ltd

THE BARBARA CARTLAND PINK COLLECTION

Barbara Cartland was the most prolific bestselling author in the history of the world. She was frequently in the Guinness Book of Records for writing more books in a year than any other living author. In fact her most amazing literary feat was when her publishers asked for more Barbara Cartland romances, she doubled her output from 10 books a year to over 20 books a year, when she was 77.

She went on writing continuously at this rate for 20 years and wrote her last book at the age of 97, thus completing 400 books between the ages of 77 and 97.

Her publishers finally could not keep up with this phenomenal output, so at her death she left 160 unpublished manuscripts, something again that no other author has ever achieved.

Now the exciting news is that these 160 original unpublished Barbara Cartland books are ready for publication and they will be published by Barbaracartland.com exclusively on the internet, as the web is the best possible way to reach so many Barbara Cartland readers around the world.

The 160 books will be published monthly and will be

numbered in sequence.

The series is called the Pink Collection as a tribute to Barbara Cartland whose favourite colour was pink and it became very much her trademark over the years.

The Barbara Cartland Pink Collection is published only on the internet. Log on to www.barbaracartland.com to find out how you can purchase the books monthly as they are published, and take out a subscription that will ensure that all subsequent editions are delivered to you by mail order to your home.

If you do not have access to a computer you can write for information about the Pink Collection to the following address :

Barbara Cartland.com Ltd.
240 High Road,
Harrow Weald,
Harrow HA3 7BB
United Kingdom.

Telephone & fax: +44 (0)20 8863 2520

THE LATE DAME BARBARA CARTLAND

Barbara Cartland who sadly died in May 2000 at the age of nearly 99 was the world's most famous romantic novelist who wrote 723 books in her lifetime with worldwide sales of over 1 billion copies and her books were translated into 36 different languages.

As well as romantic novels, she wrote historical biographies, 6 autobiographies, theatrical plays, books of advice on life, love, vitamins and cookery. She also found time to be a political speaker and television and radio personality.

She wrote her first book at the age of 21 and this was called *Jigsaw*. It became an immediate bestseller and sold 100,000 copies in hardback and was translated into 6 different languages. She wrote continuously throughout her life, writing bestsellers for an astonishing 76 years. Her books have always been immensely popular in the United States, where in 1976 her current books were at numbers 1 & 2 in the B. Dalton bestsellers list, a feat never achieved before or since by any author.

Barbara Cartland became a legend in her own lifetime and will be best remembered for her wonderful romantic novels, so loved by her millions of readers throughout the world.

Her books will always be treasured for their moral message, her pure and innocent heroines, her good looking and dashing heroes and above all her belief that the power of love is more important than anything else in everyone's life.

"Forever is a very long time, but true love lasts even longer."

Barbara Cartland

CHAPTER ONE
1870

Davina Shelford gazed from her window at the carriage drawn up in the driveway below. It had been ordered for her father, Lord Shelford. The driver sat hunched on his box, while Reeper the footman stood in almost regal attendance at the carriage door.

Davina thought Reeper looked remarkably composed, considering the fact that rain was dripping down his face with steady monotony.

At last Lord Shelford hurried down the steps and into the carriage.

Reeper closed the door after him carefully and stood back. Davina gave a wan smile as her father leaned out of the carriage window and raised his hand in farewell. Then the driver raised his whip, the horses jerked up their damp heads and the carriage set off.

Davina sank back down onto her chaise-longue and picked up the book she had been reading. After a few minutes, however, she threw it aside and sprang to her feet.

She began to pace the floor restlessly, hearing with half an ear the hem of her morning gown rustling on the thick pile carpet. That and the patter of rain at the window were the only sounds in the room.

It was too cruel of her father to forcibly ensconce her here in his new acquisition, Priory Park! She knew how proud he was at having finally purchased a proper country retreat but, as far as she was concerned, it was a retreat too far!

All because Papa had became a Lord, Davina thought miserably.

Lord Shelford, as he was now known, had made his money in steel.

He already owned a grand London house, in Curzon Street, but once he was made a peer of the realm he felt he really should have a large country estate as well. He bought Priory Park, which had stood empty for many years, and had spent a great deal of money returning it to its former glory.

Davina crossed to the window again and stared glumly out. It was not that she didn't appreciate the beauty of the countryside. She did. When her mother was alive, the family often used to spend the summers outside of London. They had a house in Kent, known as the Garden of England because it was so full of orchards.

Davina remembered a nearby farm, where she had witnessed a chicken hatch from its shell. She had watched dairy maids milking the cows and had even been permitted to churn the butter. Every afternoon she and her sister Regine took tea on the lawn with their mother. Scones and strawberry jam, with fresh cream from the farm. Mama had sipped her tea from a delicate china teacup while relating wonderful fairy tales.

They had been perfect holidays, but they were *then* and this was *now*. Then she was a child and unaware of other interests. Now she was – well, now she was nineteen and had tasted the delicious pleasure of being the *belle of the ball*.

She turned and regarded her reflection in the pier

glass. Being the belle of the ball was something of a mystery to Davina, dependent as it was on attributes she was only half aware that she possessed.

She gazed at herself with the trace of a frown. Her pale gold hair was loose on her shoulders and looked rather tangled this morning. Her nose was just *too* retroussé and her violet eyes were far too wide apart for her liking.

What *was* all the fuss about when she walked into a room? Davina could not grasp that it was precisely this lack of vanity, this spirited freshness, that made her stand out amidst all the self-regarding London beauties. Neither was she aware of how beautifully she moved, gliding across ballroom floors and drawing rooms like a ballerina.

Davina sighed and turned away from the pier glass. Her head may not have been turned by her success in London, but it *had* been turned by Felix Boyer, one of the leading actors of the day. She had listened breathlessly as Felix quoted poetry to her, grasping her milk-white hand in his.

She had swooned under his ardent gaze as he murmured words of endearment. She had gazed rapturously at him on stage as he performed all the great roles. He was so dashing and romantic!

Why, oh, why, had her father disapproved so? Why, oh, why, had he insisted she leave London and come down here to isolated Priory Park?

Would it have mattered *so* much if she had fallen in love with an actor? She knew her father was ambitious for his two daughters but surely the fact that his elder daughter, Regine, was now engaged to a Duke would allow him to be more lenient regarding Davina's romantic choice? Did he really need Davina to marry for status as well?

What Davina could not know – and what Lord Shelford could not bring himself to tell her – was that Felix

Boyer was known to gaze ardently at *any* young woman with a fortune. This despite the fact that he had been keeping a mistress in Hove for over ten years!

Davina stared around her sitting room. Her father had taken great care to have the room decorated in a way that would appeal to her and she had to admit that it was very pretty indeed. For a *prison*!

Davina walked to the door and opened it. The corridor outside was silent. She longed for the sound of voices, scurrying feet, the clip clop of horses' hooves on the London streets.

Her father was travelling to London today and would be gone for a week. He planned to meet Regine's fiancé and discuss their wedding.

Davina had wanted to go with him but to her chagrin her father had refused.

Lord Shelford had, in fact, been warned that Felix Boyer was to be seen about town in the company of a new young lady, the daughter of a Duke.

Lord Shelford did not want Davina hurt at the idea that Felix had forgotten her so soon.

Davina wandered along the south corridor, glancing through the open doors of unoccupied rooms. She had seen very little of Priory Park since she arrived. It seemed enormous to her. Her new ladies' maid, Jess, had told her there were over fifty rooms! It had two wings, an east wing and a west wing, and a great sweeping staircase leading to the upper floors. It also boasted a handsome ballroom.

Davina wondered if they would ever know enough people in the local society to fill it. This part of England seemed so far from what she considered to be civilisation. Why, this was 1870, and yet the nearest railway station was a four-hour carriage drive away! The land beyond the confines of Priory Park looked wild and lonely, composed of heathery moor and deep black lakes.

There could be nobody remotely interesting in this – this bandit country, thought Davina!

She heard footsteps ahead and a moment later Jess appeared carrying a pile of fresh linen. The maid looked anxious when she saw Davina in the corridor.

"Oh, miss, have you been looking for me? I am sure I never heard you ring."

"That is because I didn't," smiled Davina. "So please don't worry."

Jess bobbed a grateful curtsy. "I was on my way to your room to help you dress," she said.

Davina nodded absently. "Where does that corridor lead?" she asked.

Jess followed her mistress's gaze. "To the stairs that lead down to the laundry room. Or up to the attic of the east wing, miss," she added.

Davina nodded. "Who sleeps up there?"

"The laundry maid is all, miss. The main servants' quarters is above the west wing. Though I heard Lord Shelford say he were going to put some new beds up in the east attic when he hires more staff. It's early days yet, isn't it, miss?"

"Yes, it is." Davina sighed. "My father is going to need a lot more staff to run this place, I think."

Jess thought that Lord Shelford could afford it. The amount he had already spent doing up Priory Park after all its years of neglect! She could not say this, of course, so after a moment's silence she asked what she considered to be the most pressing question.

"So are you coming back to your room to dress now, miss?"

Davina shook her head. "I am going to explore a little.

I've been here over two weeks and I still feel I need a map to find my way around."

"But you're still in your morning gown, miss!" exclaimed Jess in astonishment.

"I know," laughed Davina. "And there's the clock beginning to strike noon and I should by rights be in my afternoon dress. But who is there here to see me?"

Jess stared after her mistress as she tripped off along the corridor that led to the east wing. She shook her head. Miss Davina was so pale and fragile-looking but she certainly had an unexpected will of her own.

The notes of the hall clock below echoed faintly through the house as Davina moved quickly along the corridor. She came to the narrow stairway and paused. She had no desire to descend to the steamy laundry room. She knew what she would find there. Maids pummelling garments in the big sink or hoisting them on the ceiling racks to dry.

No, she would climb the stairs to the attic.

She was breathless by the time she arrived at the top and found herself in yet another corridor. This was not as wide as the corridors below. The windows were tiny and so begrimed she could not see out of them clearly.

There was little of interest up here after all. Some of the rooms contained furniture – a crooked chest of drawers here, an iron bedstead there, a jug and basin on a stand for the laundry maids – but mostly they were empty and made her feel somehow desolate.

She wondered for the first time why Priory Park had remained abandoned for so long before her father bought it.

At the end of the corridor she came across a door that was closed.

She tried to push it open and almost cried out as the door, rotten with woodworm, came away at its hinges and simply fell to the floor with a thud.

Heart pounding, she peered into the room and saw that it was fully and indeed had once been comfortably, furnished. In the dim light she could make out a faded plush sofa and an oak table covered in a red baize cloth that was now rather moth-eaten.

When Davina saw a wicker cot in the corner, she realised this room must once have been a nursery.

It was another moment before Davina noticed a painting leaning against the wall. She walked over and picked it up.

Carrying the painting to the window, she examined it in the grey light.

She had to wipe the dust off with her sleeve before she could see the features of a melancholy but beautiful young woman staring back at her.

The young woman had rich, dark hair and large, dreamy eyes. She was obviously wealthy, for she wore diamonds at her neck. Her garments suggested that the picture had been painted in the earlier part of the century – in the 1830's, perhaps.

There was no name attached to inform her as to who the young woman might be. However, the long window behind her, with its distinctive stained glass, indicated that she had sat for the painting in the library of Priory Park.

Davina was intrigued by the young woman's mournful expression. Here surely was someone also suffering the pangs of lost love! Perhaps her lover had left her to win his fortune and never returned. Perhaps her father had refused his permission for her to marry. Whatever story lay behind the portrait, Davina was convinced it was to do with romance.

'Maybe *she* felt a prisoner in this house, just like me,' thought Davina with a dramatic thrill.

She determined to rescue the young woman from the obscurity of this forgotten room. She would hang the painting in her own bedchamber and look at it every day.

The painting was only about two foot square but the frame was heavy.

Davina looked about for a bell pull to summon help, but when she saw the rusty bell, hanging half off the wall, she knew immediately that it no longer worked.

She would have to carry the painting down herself. Jess looked up in amazement as her mistress staggered in through the door with her dusty burden.

"Bless me, miss, what have you got there?"

"I was hoping you would be able to tell *me* that, Jess," replied Davina breathlessly. She turned the frame round so that the painting was visible and propped it up on the chaise-longue. "There!" she said triumphantly, gesturing for Jess to look. "Isn't she beautiful?"

When Jess did not reply, Davina turned to look at her in surprise. Jess's face was set grimly and her eyes had narrowed.

"I've seen better," she muttered.

Davina put her head on one side. "But – do you know who she is?"

"I can give a fair guess, miss."

"So – who is she, Jess?"

Jess suddenly looked uncomfortable. "Can't say, miss."

"Can't or won't?" asked Davina, raising an eyebrow.

Jess pursed her lips and stared at the floor.

"Well," shrugged Davina after a pause, "even if she has to remain a mystery, I am still going to have her hung in my dressing room."

Jess suddenly came to alarmed life. "That's asking for

bad luck, that is, miss."

Davina was perplexed. "Bad luck?"

Jess sniffed sullenly. "That's all I'm saying, miss."

Davina regarded Jess gravely and then walked to the bell pull.

"I am going to ask for someone to come and hang the portrait for me," she asserted firmly. "I am not going to be dissuaded by any – superstitious nonsense."

Jess stood in silence as Davina tugged on the bell pull. There was nothing more she could do to prevent her young mistress from keeping this painting, but of one thing she was certain.

Davina would live to rue the day!

*

By mid-afternoon the weather had improved enough for Davina to take a drive out in her horse and trap, accompanied by Jess.

Determined to see something of the neighbourhood, Davina drove along the driveway to the gates of the estate.

The gates were locked and there was no sign of the gatekeeper.

"He's not there," said Jess, returning to the trap after having been sent to knock at the lodge door.

Davina frowned. She climbed down from the trap and walked to the gates, where she stood staring out through the bars.

'It's too bad of Papa,' she thought. 'Did he really think I would drive all the way to the station and get on the train to London?'

She was about to turn away from the gates, when she heard the sound of hooves on the road beyond. Two gentlemen came into view, trotting on a pair of shining black stallions.

Davina was struck by the visage of one of the gentlemen. He reminded her so much of Felix Boyer! Her father would have remarked that the resemblance lay in the stranger's weak mouth and soft blue eyes, but Davina saw only his fair hair and open, handsome face.

She barely noticed his companion until the two men drew abreast of the gate. Then she saw that the other was as unlike Felix as it was possible to be. He had dark, serious eyes and almost stern features. There seemed indeed to be a great deal of gravity in his expression. His hair was jet black and his skin was burnished, as if he had spent time under foreign skies.

The gentleman who reminded her of Felix slowed his horse to a walk when he saw Davina. He swept off his hat with a flourish and gave her such a broad, bright smile that she blushed.

His companion barely inclined his head in polite greeting.

The riders passed on and Davina turned to Jess, who had been standing by the trap all the while.

"Do you know those gentlemen?" she asked.

Jess nodded. "They're the young masters, miss, who live at Lark House. My cousin works there as under-maid. They are your nearest neighbours," she added.

"And yet they have not called on us!" exclaimed Davina."

"They don't call on anyone lately, miss."

Davina looked at her with interest. "Why is that?"

"Not sure, miss. Their father, Lord Delverton, died early this year, maybe that's why. Master Charles – the older, dark haired one – he is the new Lord Delverton. He came back from Africa for the funeral."

"Africa!"

"Yes, miss. He'd gone out there to run a diamond mine that he'd inherited from some distant relation. He was out there for – oh – eight years. But from what I hear, the mine failed and he lost a lot of money."

"What about his brother?" asked Davina.

"Master Howard? My cousin says he's a charmer. When old Lord Delverton took sick, Master Howard ran the estate. So I don't know how he feels about Master Charles coming back and taking over."

"Is he – is either of them – married?"

Jess suppressed a smirk. "No, miss. Nor spoken for neither."

Although Jess had done her best to hide her amusement at Davina's question, Davina was still able to divine her maid's reaction. She tossed her head as she climbed back into the trap. "Not that I have any interest. But it's good to know that if we ever have a party at Priory Park, there are at least one or two unattached gentlemen to invite."

She was about to take up the reins, when the gatekeeper appeared around the side of the lodge, in company with a swarthy fellow in a red waistcoat.

The two men were deep in conversation but stopped in their tracks when they saw the two young women. The gatekeeper stepped forward while his companion stood back in the shadows, a gun slung carelessly over his shoulder.

"I hope you're not wanting the gates opened, mistress," said the gatekeeper defensively. "I was told by his Lordship to keep 'em locked, unless there was visitors."

"Why?" demanded Davina, convinced it was to stop her fleeing to London and the arms of Felix Boyer.

It was the gatekeeper's companion who replied, stepping out of the shadows to do so.

"Why, to protect your pretty self," he said with a leer.

11

"There's been a number of robberies around here recently."

Davina felt uncomfortable under the man's black gaze. Without a word she took up the reins and turned the trap around.

"Is that true, Jess?" she asked as they set off back along the drive.

"About the robberies?"

"I did hear, miss," replied Jess, "that some carriages were attacked on the Lalham road. And there were intruders up at Caddleford Manor."

It was a moment before Davina spoke again. "And that man with the gatekeeper. Does he work for us?"

"Jed Barker? Bless me, no. He – he works for the Masters Delverton, if he works for anyone."

"You mean – Charles and – and Howard?"

"Yes, miss. He's like their – foster brother. He was found when he was about three years of age, wandering around the gardens of Lark House.

"No one came forward to claim him, so Lord Delverton called him Jed and paid the widow of a farmer on his estate to bring him up. The boy took her surname, Barker. She had no children of her own and Jed grew up playing with both the young masters Delverton, though he were always the closest to Howard."

At this, Davina's forehead puckered for an instant.

It was hard to associate the baleful Jed with the handsome, charming Howard Delverton!

She shook the reins, urging the horse on. She was not sure if it was the fresh air or the thought of Howard, but her face suddenly felt as if it was burning.

For the rest of the drive back there was only one thing on her mind. How soon would she encounter Howard Delverton again?

Davina's face might have burned even more fiercely had she known that her name arose at Lark House later that evening.

Aunt Sarah Delverton, who lived five miles away at Locksley Place, had come to visit her nephews for a few days. She and Howard were playing cards at a table drawn up near the fire. Charles sat at a desk in the far corner, poring over the accounts. At last he gave a sigh and rested his head in his hand.

Aunt Sarah glanced at her elder nephew over her cards.

"Why don't you put all that work away and join us?" she suggested. "All work and no play makes Jack a dull boy."

Charles raised his head. "While all play and no work makes Jack a *poor* boy, aunt," he countered.

Howard threw down his cards angrily. "That remark is aimed at *me*!" he cried.

"Now, now," soothed Aunt Sarah. "Charles is merely expressing his concern over the finances of the estate."

"No, he isn't," said Howard, a sullen cast over his handsome face. He was not at all pleased that his elder brother had returned to 'rule the roost' now their father was dead. "He is letting me know that he thinks I didn't work hard enough when he was away. Away having a fine time in Africa."

Charles gave a rueful smile. "I would hardly describe my experiences there as a fine time."

"Well, they must have been, otherwise why didn't you come home when father took ill? *I* had to take care of the estate business single-handed!"

"I could not return at that time," replied Charles

patiently. "It was a crucial period at the mine, when we really thought we had made a breakthrough. And that would have meant that the future of Lark House would be secure."

"But you *didn't* make a breakthrough, did you?" Howard pointed out cruelly.

Charles sighed. "No. Which is why it was so important that the finances of this estate were kept in as good an order as possible."

"There you go again!" Howard exploded. "Insinuating!"

"Insinuating?" Charles picked up a sheaf of receipts. "Then can you explain these? Receipts and bills for everything from tailors to vintners. Hotel bills and club bills. There's even a bill here for a racehorse. A racehorse! I suppose it was Jed who inveigled you into that particular purchase?"

"Leave Jed out of this. You've always had a grievance against Jed."

"My only grievance is that he has too much influence over you. Though I don't imagine you needed much influencing when it came to the rest of these bills. Hand-made boots from Italy and hand-made saddles from Spain. Hats and cloaks and hand-stitched gloves. With all this buying when did you have time for working?"

"A fellow has to look good around town," muttered Howard. "After all, that's the way we might get ourselves out of this mess."

Charles raised an eyebrow. "Exactly how would cavorting about in expensive clothes get us out of this mess?"

Howard shook his head. "My, but you are a fool! All that time in the heat of Africa has addled your brains. Has it never occurred to you that we could *marry* ourselves out of penury? There are a great many unattached heiresses floating about London like sycamore seeds. Ours for the taking."

Charles slumped back in his chair and stared at his brother. "I had no idea that you had so lost all sense of pride," he said at last.

Howard snorted. "Pride can go to the devil, brother. Pride will not pay the bills."

"Let me make one thing clear, Howard," Charles answered. "I will not have what little money remains spent on – on bounty hunting in London!"

"I am tired of having you dictate what I do," growled Howard. "Since your return you've turned us all into hermits. We go nowhere, see no one, accept no invitations, invite no one here."

"We cannot afford invitations that we can't return," insisted Charles. "We simply do not have the money to entertain on the scale you have unfortunately led people to expect of Lark House."

"Well, see here, I've had enough!" cried Howard sullenly. "I'll take myself off to London for the season and try my luck there."

Charles tightened his jaw. "At the gaming tables, no doubt!"

Aunt Sarah had been listening to this heated exchange with growing dismay. "I do wish you boys would not quarrel so," she pleaded. "What would your father say if he could hear you now? And Charles, your brother has a point. It is perfectly acceptable to marry for money."

"If I cannot support a wife on my own money, then I will not marry at all," announced Charles firmly.

Aunt Sarah shook her head. "Oh, that's – that's so silly. But Howard is being somewhat silly too. I do not see why he thinks it necessary to go all the way to London to find a wife. Particularly when there's such a splendid catch nearer home."

"What do you mean?" asked Howard, all ears suddenly.

"Why, didn't you know, Priory Park has been bought by Lord Shelford? He is a very wealthy man and his younger daughter Davina is unattached. I believe she's at the Park now."

Howard remembered the girl at the gates of Priory Park earlier.

"I think we've seen her already, he said. "A pretty thing, rather pale. Unattached, eh?" He was instantly cheered by this information and began to whistle under his breath.

Charles regarded him with distaste but decided to say no more. He picked up his pen and turned back to his accounts. Aunt Sarah, relieved that the quarrel was over, began to tidy the cards.

Howard rose to his feet. He wandered over to the mantelpiece and took a cigar from a box. He leaned down to light it at the fire, took a deep puff, and breathed out the smoke. He watched it curl in the air for a moment and then gave a little chuckle.

'Davina Shelford,' he murmured to himself. 'Davina Shelford. Well, she'll do, if I don't find better in London.'

Had Davina heard these sentiments, she would have been mortified. As it was, she lay dreaming of a young man who was the image of Felix Boyer, sweeping off his hat to her as he rode so elegantly by.

CHAPTER TWO

Two days later the *London Gazette* arrived in the post at Priory Park. Lord Shelford always read the paper at breakfast and commented on its contents to his daughter.

In the absence of her father, Davina opened the paper and spread it out on the table to read herself.

She was taking a spoonful of bramble jelly for her toast when her hand stopped in mid-air. An announcement had caught her eye.

Mr. Felix Boyer to wed the daughter of the Duke of Scrimpton. Splat! The jam dropped from its spoon and landed on the word 'wed'. She had barely been out of London for two weeks and Felix had found someone else.

All her father's hints of Felix's unworthiness as a suitor flooded Davina's mind and she suddenly felt very foolish.

How could she ever have imagined that she could compete with all those sophisticated women who swarmed the theatre foyers of London?

How could she ever have imagined that a man as worldly as Felix would be genuinely interested in her?

She wiped a tear from the corner of her eye. How humiliating to be so trifled with!

She sat for a moment longer and then a thought made her sit up.

One tear! She had shed only one tear. There was no sign of another. She screwed her eyes up to be sure, but they remained defiantly dry.

She scraped the jam from the word 'wed' and then folded the newspaper carefully for her father's return.

She returned to her room and hummed to herself as Jess dressed her hair for the day.

Jess kept her eyes low so as not to have to look at the portrait of the mournful young woman that now hung above the dressing table.

"You're cheerful, Miss Davina," she commented.

"I certainly am," replied Davina merrily. "I even feel I am going to like it here at Priory Park after all."

Jess twisted a golden tress at the nape of Davina's neck. "Might that be because you now know you have a charming neighbour?" she asked.

Her eyes met Davina's innocently in the mirror and Davina blushed.

"Well," she said after a moment, "at least it means there will be someone to dance with. If we *ever* have a ball."

Jess teased her no more but Davina's thoughts had darkened a little.

Was she really so shallow as to change her mind about a place because she had discovered that a handsome young man lived nearby? Was she really so fickle as to have shed only one tear over a gentleman with whom she had once been convinced she was falling in love?

Did she even know what love was? She had always thought it was the flutter of your heart when someone looked at you, the flush in your cheeks when someone took your hand.

Supposing it was more than that? Supposing it was something that she had never experienced at all?

18

"Jess."

"Yes, miss?"

"What – what is love, exactly?"

Jess gave a bray of laughter. "Love, miss? The *eager fly*, that's what love is."

Davina's eyes widened. "The – the eager fly?"

"Yes, miss. The fly that can't wait to get to the sugar. He lands, tastes and then he's away."

Davina's brow furrowed. "But – if your fly is a *he,* where is the *she* in your story?"

"It's no story, miss, and the *she* is the sugar. Just the sugar."

Davina said no more. She was struggling with the idea of herself as just the sugar.

That was probably all she had ever been to Felix.

Well, she was not going to let herself be the sugar again. She would not be trifled with by any man, that was for sure!

She stood and held up her arms while Jess slipped her day dress over her head. As Jess hooked up the back, Davina watched a ray of bright sunlight stream across the carpet and dapple her feet.

"It's too beautiful to stay indoors," she said.

Since she could not take the trap out of the estate, Davina decided she would take a walk in the grounds.

Jess declined to accompany her. Her mistress was perfectly safe within the confines of the park and besides, if there was one thing Jess disliked more than eager flies, it was using her feet to no purpose. If you were not walking on an errand or to accomplish a chore, what was the point?

Davina was perfectly happy to be left to explore alone. She put an apple in her silk purse and set off. The air was so balmy she hardly needed her shawl.

She strolled to the edge of the lake that lay to the south of the house.

The water was as still as glass and a lone swan glided on its blue surface.

She walked right around the lake to the other side and looked back at Priory Park from this vantage point.

The house was large and imposing but she still felt there was something a little forbidding about its exterior. As if it had originally been built by someone more interested in power and prestige than in beauty and harmony.

Yet she was distinctly aware that she liked it today more than she had yesterday.

It was now noon and the sun at its zenith was merciless. Davina wished she had brought something to drink. She remembered her apple and, taking it from her purse, began to munch happily.

A rustling sound behind her made her turn.

She was gazing down an overgrown pathway that ran into a cool, green wood. A small deer stood trembling in her view. For a moment its liquid eyes settled on Davina. Then it shot away, its white bobtail vanishing amid the trees.

Davina followed, drawn as much by the idea of sweet shade as by curiosity as to where the path led.

It was man-made, a series of stones twisting and turning round the roots of evergreens and still vaguely visible beneath a layer of moss.

Finally she came to a clump of hawthorn that had grown right across the path. Forcing her way through she found herself in a little glade. In the centre of the glade was a tombstone, horizontal in the grass. Across its inscription lay a fresh bunch of wild flowers. Intrigued, Davina pushed the flowers aside to read, EVELYN FELK, ERRANT WIFE, BORN 1815 DIED 1837.

She barely had time to muse on this find when a gust of wind shook the bushes and trees around her like rag dolls. Everything seemed to be in sudden, wild motion. The glade had darkened and peering up through the boughs she saw that angry black clouds were racing across the sun.

With one more glance at the name on the tombstone, Davina lifted her skirts and stumbled through the bushes. It was too gloomy to make out the path and so she zig-zagged through the trees with only her own instinct to guide her.

Alas, it was not enough! Bursting from the cover, she found herself on an unfamiliar tract of land. There was no lake and no house, only open field and sky.

Rather than go back into the wood, seeming more impenetrably dark by the minute, she decided to skirt the trees hoping to find her way back to the lake that way.

After fifteen minutes of hurrying through the long grass she faltered.

Perhaps she was going the wrong way? Perhaps she should turn back and skirt the trees in the opposite direction?

When she turned, however, she was facing the wind. It whipped her cheeks and tugged at her skirt and shawl. She clamped a hand to her bonnet and struggled forward. The cold made her eyes stream and, worse, she felt the first few drops of threatened rain.

'I am going to get drenched and cold and – I'll be lost forever,' she shivered. As a low branch lashed at her face, she screamed and spun aside from the trees.

Facing the horizon, she saw to her unbounded relief, the figure of a horse and rider wheel about at her cry and come galloping towards her over the field. When she recognised the steed as a black stallion her heart lifted even higher.

It was Howard Delverton come to rescue her, she was certain!

Such a fierce blast of wind suddenly stung her eyes that she had to lower her head and keep it lowered. She was using all her strength now to remain upright.

When the stallion arrived at her side she could not look upon the rider's face. But she was aware of the strong arms that reached down and lifted her up in one sweep to the saddle, heard the strong, commanding voice as it urged the stallion to stay steady. One hand clasped Davina's waist and she sank with relief against the firm, masculine frame behind her.

"We are in for a bad storm," her saviour cried above the wind. "May I ask whither you are bound, madam?"

"P-Priory Park," she stammered as loudly as she could.

Her companion wheeled his horse round and they set off at a gallop. In a moment she saw a high fence appear to their right.

"You had left the boundary of Priory Park estate," her companion cried.

"Rather than return through the wood, I am going to jump the fence. Hold tight."

The horse and its two riders soared through the air. She felt herself gripped against Howard's breast and closed her eyes with an unexpected sense of ecstasy. She was barely aware when they landed. Her heart was beating loudly, but not with fear.

The lake was soon in view. Horse and riders raced towards the house and reached it just as the thin drops of rain turned into large icy hailstones.

The horse was guided straight up the steps of the terrace and in under the protruding shelter of the portico. Its rider leapt from the saddle and turned to help Davina down. She saw his face for the first time and froze.

It was not Howard Delverton at all! It was his elder brother, Charles.

The grave one, the serious one, with the dark eyes.

Charles regarded her with what she thought was impatience.

"Well, madam, do you wish to descend?"

"I-I'm sorry," she gasped. "I do, of course."

His hands grasped her waist and she felt herself lifted carefully to the ground. She stood speechless before her rescuer, aware that her eyes still streamed and that her bonnet was askew. For a moment, Charles gazed gravely at her. Then, with a sudden reach of his hand, he gently straightened her bonnet, after which he gave her a slight bow.

"I trust you are no worse the wear for your adventure," he said.

"N-no. I must thank you for your help. Please – can I offer you some refreshment?"

"Thank you, no. I must ride on home or my aunt will imagine I am drowned."

For the first time Davina was aware of the hail drumming on the portico roof.

"B-but you may well be drowned, if you venture on in this deluge!"

"This? A deluge?" Charles smiled, almost grimly. "This is nothing compared to the rains of Africa! The hail there could stun an elephant."

With another bow he leapt into his saddle. He raised a hand in farewell, dug his heels into the steaming flank of his horse, and was gone.

Davina drew in against the wall, wondering.

She could not have imagined Felix Boyer acting with such authority.

She was not even sure that Howard, so similar in his demeanour to Felix, would have behaved in such a commanding way. She had felt so – so safe in Charles Delverton's hands.

It was a new sensation for Davina.

Looking up, she saw the butler gaping at her from one of the French doors that opened from the terrace into the drawing room. He had obviously seen her arrive on the black stallion.

The afternoon had grown so dark that the lamps were being lit and the butler held a burning taper in his hand as he hastily opened the door for Davina to enter.

Davina nodded a greeting, shook out her shawl and removed her bonnet, then hurried towards the hall. At the door, however, she suddenly remembered what she had seen in the wood. She paused and turned.

"Parfitt."

"Yes, miss?"

"Have you heard of the name – Felk? Evelyn Felk?"

Parfitt stared at her, unblinking. "No, miss."

Davina was not sure that she believed him, but she walked on into the hallway and ran up the stairs.

Reaching her bedchamber, she rang for Jess and then sat down before her dressing table. Her hair had come loose and fell untidily over her shoulders. The rims of her eyes were raw from the wind and her cheeks were as red as – as lobster shells. What *must* Charles have thought of her?

She took up the hairbrush and was absently drawing it through her stray curls when Jess bustled in.

"You should have waited for me, miss."

Davina sat silently for a moment, watching her maid in the mirror.

"Jess," she said, "have you ever heard the name

Evelyn Felk?"

"No, miss," said Jess quickly – too quickly, her eyes flicking for an instant at the portrait that hung above their heads.

Davina's gaze lifted to the same portrait and at once she knew. All thoughts of her recent encounter with Charles Delverton flew from her mind.

The mournful, romantic young woman depicted in the painting was surely the same young woman who was buried out in the lonely forest.

She was surely Evelyn, *errant wife*!

*

The next morning Davina awoke with a severe headache and sore throat.

She nonetheless insisted on getting dressed and repairing to the large drawing room. Her father was due back that afternoon and she had no wish to be confined to bed when he arrived.

The weather had not improved since yesterday. The sky was grey and rain pattered relentlessly at the windows. Davina felt cold and asked for a fire to be lit.

"I think you should be in bed, miss," scolded Jess, watching as one of the servants set a taper to the logs piled in the large hearth.

"Nonsense!" said Davina. "What good would that do me? I am resting as much here as I would be in bed."

"Well, if you're not better by lunch, I'm having the doctor called," grumbled Jess, tucking a rug about her mistress's knees. "His Lordship said I was to look after you."

Davina sighed and lay back on the sofa. There was a pile of books at her side, but she was content for the moment to simply gaze at the logs as they began to glow.

The events of yesterday played over in her mind. The grave in the woods and Charles Delverton had become inextricably linked in her imagination, though reason told her there could be no connection between them at all. Her heart thrilled every time she relived her rescue.

She was used to men with silver tongues and polished manners. She was used to men who smiled easily and wielded charm like a weapon. She was not at all used to men who looked grave and made no effort to impress her.

Smoke from the fire began to waft into the room and Davina wrinkled her nose, wanting to sneeze. She was searching in her reticule for a handkerchief when Parfitt appeared at the door.

"Lord Delverton has arrived to pay his respects, Miss Davina," announced Parfitt.

"L-Lord Delverton?" repeated Davina. The sudden pounding of her heart took her by surprise and her hands flew to her cheeks, which felt suddenly flushed.

Parfitt regarded her with concern. "Shall I tell him you are indisposed, Miss Davina?"

"Yes – I mean no. No. I will receive him."

He bowed with surprise and left the room. Jess opened her mouth to protest, but at a pleading look from Davina, she gave a sniff and moved to sit in the corner, a silent chaperone.

Charles Delverton, strode into the room, but stopped with a start when he saw Davina at full stretch on the sofa.

"You are – not well, madam?' he asked with concern.

Davina waved a hand as airily as she knew how. She had it in mind that Charles was used to a different species of women than she had ever encountered. The kind of women who followed their men-folk to Africa, dealing with snakes and mosquitoes and wild animals with never a word of complaint. She was determined not to appear a fragile little rich girl.

"A c-chill, Lord D-Delverton. Nothing at all. I am s-so pleased to see you. Do sit down."

Charles took a seat, scanning her face warily. He was struck by the brilliance of her violet eyes, shining like diamonds in the darkness of a mine, he thought.

"You – you were very gallant to me yesterday," continued Davina. "I do not know how to thank you."

Charles inclined his head. "I did what any gentleman would have done in the circumstance, madam."

"I am – sure that is not the case – my Lord." Davina found herself faltering under Charles's gaze. It was so severe, so very penetrating.

He must have a good deal of weighty matters on his mind, she thought, passing a hand across her brow.

Charles made as if to rise. "I am afraid I am tiring you, madam."

"Tiring me?" Davina made an effort to appear nonchalant. "Oh, not at all, my Lord. I was just wondering whether – whether I might ask you a question?"

"By all means."

Davina glanced over at Jess, whose head seemed to have sunk drowsily onto her chest. Then she leaned forward conspiratorially, speaking in a rapid, low voice.

"Have you ever heard the name – Evelyn Felk? Because you see yesterday I found a grave in the wood inscribed with that name. And I found a portrait in the attic and I am sure it's the same woman. Only nobody will tell me about her. Do you know the history of Priory Park? You must do if you grew up in the area. You did grow up in the area, didn't you?"

The ghost of a smile flickered on his lips.

"Which exact question is it I am to answer?" he enquired.

Davina fell back, her face heated. "Oh, I'm sorry – I do seem to be prattling on, don't I? Perhaps you could answer them all and then I would – oh! oh!"

"What is the matter?' cried Lord Delverton, rising in alarm. Jess too sprang up and gazed bewilderedly about her.

"I – I think I am going to sneeze!" wailed Davina.

Charles seemed to grasp the dilemma in an instant. He thrust his hand into his waistcoat and drew out a large handkerchief. Davina seized this article eagerly and pressed it to her face.

"*A – choo.   A – choo.   A – choo!*"

Davina thought she detected a twinkle in Lord Delverton's eye as she at last raised her head from the handkerchief.

"I am so sorry," she snuffled. "I foolishly left my handkerchief case upstairs."

"Why then, I am glad I was here to be of service," said Charles, glancing at Jess as she resumed her seat in the corner.

"Now, regarding the questions that you have asked me. I will start by telling you that I did indeed grow up in this area. My family have been settled at Lark House since the seventeenth century.

"Priory Park was built in the late 1830's or thereabouts by one Hubert, Lord Felk.

"He had it built for his young wife, your very Evelyn. However they produced no children and after their deaths the house was abandoned. My brother and I and a childhood companion used to play in the grounds and in the semi-ruins when we were boys."

"Is that – all?" she asked.

He turned from the fire. "All?"

"You – you said there was a tragedy. Was it something to do with Evelyn being an – an errant wife?"

Jess threw up her hands. "Bless me, miss, where'd you hear that? *I* didn't tell you, to be sure."

"Indeed you didn't," acknowledged Davina patiently. "It was inscribed on the grave, after her name."

She jumped as a flaming log slipped noisily sideways in the hearth.

Charles rose to take up the poker and re-arrange the fire. He stood staring down into the glow for a moment and then he spoke.

"I am afraid I do not know any other details of the story," he said. He turned and picked up his gloves, which he had left on the arm of his chair.

"I am pleased to see that you have suffered no serious after effects from your adventure yesterday. And now, madam, I must return home to my brother and aunt. I promised to join them for lunch."

He bowed politely and left the room.

Davina stared after him.

"Lord Delverton *does* know the details, I am sure of it!' she exclaimed.

"Why wouldn't he tell me, Jess?"

"Well, miss, it's a bit – a bit delicate for a gentleman to relate to a young lady."

"Oh, Jess, now I'm *too* curious!" cried Davina. "I'll die if you don't tell me! I will give you that Chinese shawl you like if you do," she added quickly.

Jess struggled with herself. She shouldn't tell, she knew she shouldn't, but she could just see herself at church of a Sunday in that lovely green shawl. And surely Miss Davina already guessed the gist of story, having read those words 'errant wife' – "I suppose there's no real harm," the maid said at last, "but you're not to let on to your father that I told you, for he instructed everyone in the house never to mention it."

"My *father* did?"

"Yes, miss. He said it wasn't a story for a young lady's ears, particularly one as sensitive as yourself."

Jess continued, "Anyway, it's like this. Lord Felk built Priory Park so as to keep his wife away from society. She was much, much younger than him, see, and he was jealous and possessive and wanted her all to himself.

"But it didn't do him no good, because soon after they started living here, Lord Felk took ill. He used to have fits, they say. And his wife, well – she took up with someone else."

"A lover!" breathed Davina.

"Yes, miss. Apparently he wasn't – of her class, but she was besotted with him, so they say. Lord Felk found out and he – shot the lover. Then he shot himself."

Davina gasped. "And what happened to Evelyn?"

"She went mad, miss. She used to wander the grounds at night, in her shift. Looking for her lover, they say."

Now that she had allowed herself to tell the story, Jess was extracting all the relish out of it that she could.

"Then one night, miss – one dark and stormy night when you couldn't see no moon nor stars – she drowned herself. In the lake."

Davina's hand flew to her mouth. "Oh – the poor creature."

"That's what you get for being errant, miss," said Jess firmly. "And there's worse. There were rumours of a – a baby."

An image came to Davina of the room where she had

30

discovered the painting. A faded plush sofa, a table covered with a moth-eaten cloth and, in a corner, a little wicker cot.

"I don't think the baby *was* a rumour, Jess," she said slowly.

"Maybe not, miss, but there was never any sign of it. A distant cousin of Lord Felk arrived and had Evelyn buried out there in the woods. Where she and her lover used to meet. The house was boarded up and left to rot. The cousin didn't want it, after what had happened here."

Jess added dramatically, "it's said that Lady Felk's ghost still haunts the grounds."

Davina shook her head wonderingly. "A ghost? Well! You certainly know a great deal about it all."

"Everyone in these parts knows about it. I suppose I might know more than most because my grandmother was a cook here under Lord Felk."

Davina sank back into the sofa, her mind reeling.

No wonder the young woman in the portrait looked so mournful. Her husband was much older and subject to fits, and had built a house in which she felt herself to be a virtual prisoner.

There was just one piece of the puzzle that Davina could not place.

All these events had taken place some thirty years before.

So who was it that, only yesterday, had placed a bunch of fresh flowers on Evelyn Felk's grave?

CHAPTER THREE

Lord Shelford arrived late afternoon. He was somewhat concerned to find Davina with a chill and desired her to retire to bed, but she was anxious to take tea with him by the fire. She wanted to hear all about London and her sister's wedding plans.

"Regine is determined to marry from our London house," said Lord Shelford. "She also wants to throw a big engagement party there next Spring."

Davina clapped her hands. "You will have to let me return to London then, Papa!"

Lord Shelford glanced at his daughter. He wondered when it would be politic to inform her of Felix Boyer's engagement. Davina caught his look and guessed what lay behind it.

"And did you see anything of Mr. Boyer?" she asked with an air of innocence.

"I can't say I did," replied her father, leaning forward to take up his cup. "He was – er – otherwise engaged."

"Yes," cried Davina mischievously. "To the daughter of a Duke!"

Lord Shelford almost spilled his tea. "What! You know?"

"I read it in your newspaper," laughed Davina. "And Papa –I don't care a bit. So you have no need to worry about me."

"What a puzzling little monkey you are!" he exclaimed.

"No, Papa," replied Davina gravely. "What is puzzling is that I should ever have imagined that I cared for him in the first place. I must be very – shallow, I think."

"Nonsense. You are young and impressionable, that's all. And Mr. Boyer is a – is a – "

"An eager fly?" prompted Davina.

"An eager fly?" repeated Lord Shelford in astonishment. "From whom did you learn such a phrase?"

"Jess," admitted Davina.

He frowned and put down his cup. "And what else has your maid been so kind as to reveal to you?"

"Oh, nothing," said Davina airily, mindful of her promise to Jess. "But Papa – I had such an adventure yesterday."

"It wouldn't be this adventure that caused your chill, I suppose?" asked her father gravely.

"Probably, Papa."

"You had better tell me all about it, then."

Davina proceeded to relate the events of the day before. She confessed to having found the grave in the wood and noticed the immediate concern on her father's face. He soon forgot about the grave, however, when she carried on to describe her rescue by Lord Delverton.

"A knight in shining armour, eh?" he mused.

"Yes indeed Papa."

Lord Shelford wondered if this knight was responsible for his daughter's equanimity on hearing the news of Felix Boyer's engagement. "Well, I shall have to call on him to thank him. And you must come along too."

"Oh, *yes*, Papa!"

Lord Shelford regarded Davina with mock severity.

"So you had better take yourself off to bed and get rid of that chill, young lady."

"I will instantly, Papa." Davina rose and kissed the top of her father's head. "I will be as good as new tomorrow, you see if I'm not!"

*

When Charles returned to Lark House after his visit to Davina, he was furious to discover from Aunt Sarah that Howard had taken advantage of his brother's absence to slip away to London.

Opening the lid of the black box on his desk, he frowned. "Howard helped himself to funds, too, aunt. How am I ever going to turn around the fortunes of this estate if he works against me in this fashion?"

Aunt Sarah looked troubled. "But he said he would turn our fortunes around – in London."

"Did he travel alone or with Jed Barker?" asked Charles wryly.

Aunt Sarah picked at a stray thread on one of her mittens. "He – he went with Jed."

"Then it's the roulette wheel that will be turning, aunt, not our fortunes."

"Oh, dear," replied Aunt Sarah. "I do hope not. He said he hoped to find himself an heiress."

"He won't be the only hunter in London in that respect," said Charles sardonically.

"Howard said you were going to visit Priory Park this morning?" she asked.

"And so I did," said Charles.

Aunt Sarah was delighted. Knowing nothing of Charles's rescue of Davina the day before, she assumed her nephew had at last decided to follow the normal practice of paying one's respect to neighbours.

"And did you meet the young lady?" she enquired.

"I did. Lord Shelford himself was absent."

Aunt Sarah gazed hopefully at Charles. "And is she as – pretty as they say she is, this Davina Shelford?"

In response, Charles found his mind flooded with a vision of Davina's upturned face as she stood with him under the portico yesterday. He saw again her flushed cheeks and the golden curls escaping from her bonnet.

Following on came another vision of her eyes that morning, as bright as diamonds and yet as violet-hued as the African sky at dusk.

These images proved so vivid and so pleasing that Charles was unexpectedly shaken. He put a hand out to steady himself and found the edge of the carved mantelpiece.

What strange twist of the heart was this? He had convinced himself that his visit to Priory Park was made out of pure courtesy. Now he had to wonder.

"Charles?" pouted Aunt Sarah.

Charles straightened. "Yes, aunt?"

"Is she pretty?"

"Yes, aunt. She is."

"And – are you visiting her again soon?"

Charles turned sharply away. "No, aunt, I am not."

Aunt Sarah was puzzled and disappointed. Why would her nephew not do the sensible thing and court a pretty young heiress?

She did not understand that Charles would as easily rip all images of Davina from his heart as offend his own sense of pride. He was firmly resolved to offer his attentions to no lady whose fortunes were in any way greater than his own.

Aunt Sarah was so exasperated with her nephew that

she determined to cut short her visit to Lark House and return home the very next day.

Her mind was changed, however, when early the next morning she saw an unfamiliar carriage rolling up to the house.

The diminutive under-maid answered the ring of the bell and stared open-mouthed up at Reeper, Lord Shelford's footman.

"Lord Shelford and Miss Davina Shelford wish pay to their respects to Lord Delverton," Reeper announced haughtily above the under-maid's head.

Aunt Sarah, listening at the drawing room door, was thrown into confusion. She was thrilled, of course, that Lord Shelford and Davina had called, but at the same time she could not but be aware of the fact that there was no longer a butler or even a doorman at Lark House. So far have the family fortunes declined, she thought in despair, as she went forth to greet the visitors.

She did not miss Lord Shelford's acute appraisal of his surroundings, even as he gave Aunt Sarah a polite bow.

Lord Shelford had guessed, from Davina's excited chatter on the way to Lark House, that Lord Delverton had indeed somewhat replaced Felix Boyer in his daughter's affections.

He was therefore keen to take the measure of Lord Delverton's general situation.

He had not failed to notice, once his carriage drove through the Lark House gates that the estate was run-down and somewhat neglected. Fences needed repairing, trees needed pruning.

Now, in the house, his eyes roved over the faded tapestries, the worn covers on the chairs, the general air of shabbiness.

Watching him, Aunt Sarah reddened. For the first time

she appreciated the reasons why Charles might not wish to invite the neighbourhood gentry into his house.

She did not realise that Lord Shelford, though quickly cognisant of the financial state of the Delverton affairs, was nonetheless impressed by the family's aristocratic lineage. His own title had been recently acquired and he secretly felt that he could not hold a candle to a *real* Lord.

This feeling was reinforced by his first sight of Lord Delverton.

Charles rose in surprise from his desk as Lord Shelford and Davina were admitted to his presence.

Lord Shelford was most favourably struck by the young man's carriage and demeanour.

'There's true blue blood for you,' he told himself with satisfaction.

Aunt Sarah motioned Davina to the sofa. Lord Shelford refused a seat and stood with his back to the fire, arms under his tailcoat.

"Fine old house you have here," he remarked cheerily.

"Thank you," said Charles. "It has been in the family for over two centuries."

Davina had sat down quietly with her eyes lowered. At the sound of Charles's voice, she raised her head. Aunt Sarah drew in her breath at the sight of those violet eyes.

What a little beauty, she thought. Why on earth is Charles so resolutely *not* looking her way?

Davina was similarly disappointed that Charles had accorded her the barest of acknowledgements. He seemed more interested in her father than in herself. He and Lord Shelford stood at the fireside discussing the recent outbreak of robberies in the area.

"I considered it remote around here," said Lord Shelford. "That is why I liked it so much. But I didn't expect such a degree of lawlessness. I have heard tell that the perpetrators of these outrages may be gypsies?"

"A band has set up camp recently, about ten miles from here," Charles conceded. "But that proves nothing."

"Hmmph," grunted Lord Shelford. "A co-incidence, all the same. It's a worry, I can tell you. I instructed my gatekeeper to keep the gates locked while I was away recently. Concerned about my little monkey here."

"Indeed," said Charles stiffly.

Davina coloured, both at being alluded to as a little monkey and then being barely glanced at by Lord Delverton.

"I understand, sir, that you were kind enough to rescue her from the storm yesterday," continued Lord Shelford.

"I was glad to be of assistance," he murmured. Still he did not look at Davina.

Aunt Sarah frowned at her nephew and turned toward Lord Shelford.

"May we offer you some tea?" she asked sweetly.

Lord Shelford shook his head. "Thank you, madam, but we won't stop. I came to convey my gratitude to Lord Delverton and to ask whether he would be so gracious as to join us at Priory Park on Saturday for supper. Needless to say the invitation is extended, madam, to your good self."

"We shall be delighted to accept," Aunt Sarah said swiftly, before her nephew could reply.

There was a pause and then Charles gave a small bow.

"Certainly and thank you," he said. "At what hour shall you expect us?"

"Oh, say seven o'clock," replied Lord Shelford. "There will be light enough to show you something of our renovations, if you are interested."

Not until she was about to pass through into the hallway did Davina turn to glance back at Charles.

With a shock, her eyes met his where they followed her departure in the mirror above the fireplace. For just a second their mutual glance held.

Then Charles looked away and Davina walked on.

All the way home to Lark House she puzzled over the expression she had glimpsed on Lord Delverton's face.

His gaze had been on her, no doubt, and that surely betokened interest. Yet his jaw had been clenched and in his eyes had flared an emotion she could never have imagined she might inspire.

That emotion was anguish and it had so struck at Davina's heart that she felt from this moment on her life was changed.

If she could not marry Lord Delverton of Lark House then she did not care who in the world she married.

*

Two days after Lord Shelford's visit, Charles glanced up from his desk and was astonished to see through the window his brother Howard and Jed Barker riding up the driveway to Lark House. He hastened outside to greet them.

"I thought you were away for the entire season?" he remarked drily as Howard dismounted.

"I – didn't do too well, brother," admitted Howard rather sheepishly.

Charles cast a look at Jed, who still sat astride his horse. Jed stared back insolently and then caught up the reins of Howard's gelding.

"I'll be off to the stable," he said. Charles watched him go and then turned to Howard.

"So how much did you lose?" he asked.

Howard grimaced. "The lot, brother."

"And no bride?" enquired Charles sarcastically.

Howard groaned. "Don't berate me, Charles, there's a good fellow. I thought I was doing the right thing."

Howard looked so woebegone that Charles said no more.

He sent a note to Lord Shelford informing him of the unexpected return of his brother. He rather hoped this news might prompt Lord Shelford to postpone the supper at Priory Park. Charles disliked the struggle that arose in his breast whenever he laid eyes on Davina.

Lord Shelford was not easily dissuaded, however. He simply invited Howard to accompany Charles and Aunt Sarah on Saturday evening.

Howard and Aunt Sarah drove to Priory Park in the family coach.

Charles followed on his own horse. He was sunk in his own thoughts all the way.

The sophisticated society women he had met before his travels had never appealed to him. The daughters of hunters and missionaries he met in Africa had appealed even less. They were admirable but unimaginative ladies, toughened by climate and experience.

Not that it would have made any difference had a single one of them touched his heart. Since his failure on that searing continent to improve the family fortune – a fortune depleted by the poor judgement of his father and the profligacy of his brother – he had steeled himself for a long bachelor-hood.

Saving what was left of the Lark House estate would consume all his energies and as such he had considered himself impervious to romance.

Now Davina Shelford, this guileless and delicate creature, had somehow penetrated his defences. He was almost angry with himself for allowing it.

These thoughts so dominated his mind that when he

arrived at Priory Park and Davina presented her hand in eager greeting, his eyes were hooded and cold.

Davina's hand was trembling as she drew it away from his lips.

This same man who had clasped her tight against his breast in the storm, who had lifted her so gently from the saddle to set her on her feet, who had straightened her bonnet on her head as she stood blushing before him – this same man now looked at her as if he wished she was not there.

His brother Howard, by contrast, made his appreciation of Davina clear from the moment he was introduced.

"How enchanting you look!" he murmured, as he took her hand. "I do hope you will allow me to lead you in to supper."

Davina was pitifully grateful for Howard's attentions. She had spent hours preparing for this evening's supper, shaking her head as Jess lay dress after dress out for her inspection.

"That one is too dull – that makes my skin look green – that makes me look ancient," she flustered.

In the end she had chosen a pale pink voile with a hem of embroidered roses. Jess had arranged two pink roses in her hair and told her she looked "like a princess in a fairy-tale, miss."

All to no avail. Lord Delverton had barely acknowledged her. She might as well have been a – a wooden umbrella stand!

To hide her distress, she responded to Howard with an almost incandescent gaiety as the evening wore on. She laughed brightly at his jokes, lowered her eyes before his searching gaze, blushed at his endless compliments.

Aunt Sarah, watching the two of them at supper, could barely contain her excitement.

If Howard was not in the process of winning that young lady's heart, she would eat her silk mittens!

She glanced at Charles with almost cruel satisfaction. Her elder nephew's eyes were dark and unreadable, but she had not failed to notice how increasingly often they strayed towards the figures of Howard and Davina.

'Serves him right if he should regret not winning her interest,' she thought. 'He should have made a move sooner.'

Davina herself, although appearing to concentrate on Howard, watched Charles longingly from under her eyebrows.

When he glanced her way, his eyes were almost black with emotion and a muscle flinched in his jaw. 'It is almost as though he – resents me,' she thought. Only then did an alternative interpretation strike her and her heart began to flutter hopefully. 'Could Lord Delverton possibly be jealous?' she wondered.

Oh, how wonderful if he was!

She almost immediately reprimanded herself. Who was she to imagine she might prove alluring to a man like Lord Delverton? He found her trivial and irritating, that was why he looked her way so darkly.

As the butler cleared the plates away, Lord Shelford once again alluded to the recent spate of robberies in the neighbourhood.

"They are indeed on the increase," Charles acknowledged. "I take the precaution now of carrying a gun with me wherever I go."

"I hear the parson was attacked on the way back from a visit to a parishioner," said Lord Shelford. "They knocked the poor fellow about a bit. Quite uncalled for! But what can you expect? These gypsies have no respect for a man of the cloth!"

For the first time, Howard's attention was drawn away from Davina.

"Who says it is the gypsies?" he asked. "I don't know why they always get the blame. They are not all devils, you know."

"I wouldn't know if they are devils or not," responded Lord Shelford hotly. "I have never had the occasion to meet or converse with any of them. But their reputation goes before them. They are loose of tongue and light of finger."

"That is a terrible generalisation, Lord Shelford," asserted Howard.

Charles agreed. "I think we must be careful not to judge these people unfairly, just because they live outside our society."

"Outside our laws, you mean," sniffed Lord Shelford.

"They have their own laws," replied Charles simply.

"They do," Howard cut in keenly. "And they keep all sorts of interesting customs. Stories are passed down through the generations. Music that makes you want to throw all your inhibitions to the wind."

"That I can believe," countered Lord Shelford dryly.

"They do have the most colourful costumes," sighed Aunt Sarah abstractedly.

The gentlemen paused politely for a moment and then continued their conversation.

Davina found her eye and ear drawn time and again to Lord Delverton.

His eyes blazed as he defended the right of the gypsies to their own long-established way of life. She could not have imagined such passion burned in his breast, for he was so outwardly composed, even severe.

She wondered longingly what it would be like to be the object of such passion.

43

Her gaze drifted to his brother, Howard.

Davina had to admit that Howard was charming and handsome. His face seemed almost boyish compared to the grave features of his brother.

Whenever he made what he thought was a good point, his eye sought out Davina as if to gauge her response.

Once or twice Howard even winked at her. For some reason this made her blush.

Parfitt circled the table, refilling glasses. Aunt Sarah's cheeks and nose began to glow. Davina drank only a little, but still she began to feel heady. It had been a fine day, but Lord Shelford had ordered a fire lit in the dining room, as the evenings often proved chilly.

Now the room was growing stuffy. She looked over at the row of French windows. The curtains had still not been drawn but the doors were all shut tight. Perhaps one of them should be opened to let in a little fresh air?

"I think there is a good deal too much nonsense talked about the rights of these people," began Lord Shelford, when he was interrupted by a piercing scream from Davina.

Charles leapt to his feet, as Davina rose shaking from her chair.

"Good God, madam, what is the matter?" he cried.

Davina lifted stricken eyes to his and then appeared to swoon. He was at her side in an instant, moving so swiftly that Howard and Lord Shelford barely had time to register what was happening.

Charles swept Davina into his arms and carried her to a chaise longue near the fire.

"Water, someone," he commanded.

Aunt Sarah, pale and wide-eyed, filled a glass from the water jug and hurried to the chaise. Charles took the glass and raised it to Davina's lips.

"Drink, my dar – drink, Davina," he urged.

As Davina obeyed, her eyes and his locked. At such close quarters, his ardent concern could not be concealed. For an instant his hand rose as if to sweep her curls from her forehead. Then he seemed to recollect himself. He stood and moved to one side as Lord Shelford knelt by the chaise.

"What was it, my dear daughter? What did you see?"

Davina closed her eyes and shuddered. "There was a – face. At the window. Staring eyes and white, wild hair. It was the ghost! I am sure it was the ghost!"

"Now, now." Lord Shelford patted his daughter's hand. "What ghost are you talking about?"

"The ghost of – Evelyn Felk."

Lord Shelford frowned. "Now this is exactly why I did not want you hearing those stories. You've too vivid an imagination, my girl."

"But there *was* a face!" wailed Davina.

"Lord Shelford," said Charles, "permit me to go and search the grounds. That will surely lay this – ghost to rest."

"A good idea," nodded Lord Shelford. "I will ring for a lamp."

A servant brought a lamp and Charles departed. Davina sat up and drank some more water. She was still pale and had started to shiver but she would not retire until Lord Delverton came back from his search.

Lord Shelford rang for Jess to bring a shawl, which Howard then insisted on taking to wrap around Davina's shoulders. She smiled at him wanly but did not speak.

Charles returned after twenty minutes. His hair was damp and a lock fell over his forehead.

"I saw no one," he revealed.

Lord Shelford was about to pronounce himself vindicated when Charles raised a hand to silence him.

"However, I did find footprints in the wet clay to the side of the French window. Somebody was there all right."

Howard gave a low whistle. "Who do you suppose it was?"

"I can tell you who it was," cried Lord Shelford. "One of the robbers, that's who!"

There was silence for a moment. Davina shrank fearfully into her shawl.

"That is a distinct possibility," said Charles at last.

"Oh, dear!" broke out Aunt Sarah. "My house has been empty all this time, just the servants about, and they are hopeless in a crisis. Supposing I have been robbed in my absence? I want to go home! I want to go home!"

"What, tonight, aunt?" asked Howard.

"Yes, tonight," wailed the old lady. "But supposing I am robbed on the way?"

Charles took his aunt's hand between his own.

"Calm down, Aunt Sarah," he said kindly. "I will escort you home and then ride on to Lalham to catch the train to London. I had intended to go on business and might as well leave tonight."

Howard ran a finger over his lip thoughtfully. "How long will you be away, Charles?"

"Oh, a fortnight or so," he replied.

Davina felt crushed. A fortnight! A fortnight was as good as forever.

That moment of intimacy with Lord Delverton – his coming so swiftly to her rescue a second time – had begun to make her think he cared for her in the way she wished. Now he was going to London, a city of myriad distractions.

How could she ensure that he did not forget her?

She swallowed. "L-Lord Delverton?"

"Madam?"

Davina blushed. "I should – like to hear news of London – while you are away," she murmured.

Charles hesitated. He knew what she was asking for and it went against his resolve. How could he withstand the emotion she aroused in him if he corresponded with her while he was away?

Aunt Sarah had no such considerations. As far as she was concerned, whether Davina succumbed to Howard or Charles was immaterial. Either of them as groom would have the same beneficial effect on the coffers of the family. She was well aware of Howard looking daggers at his brother, but she did not care. All fires should be fanned, was her philosophy.

"My nephew will be delighted to write to you, Miss Davina," she said firmly. "Won't you, Charles?"

He might have been amused at his aunt's tenacity had it not struck when he felt at his weakest, under the beseeching gaze of this alluring Davina Shelford. However, he could prevaricate no longer. He gave a short bow of assent.

"It will be my pleasure," he said.

"You – you promise?" Davina breathed.

"I promise," Charles replied. "Now, aunt, I think it is time we departed, if I am to return you home tonight."

Their carriage was ordered. The little party gathered in the hall to say their goodbyes, Davina leaning on her father's arm. Howard was riding back to Lark House alone. He kissed Davina's hand, his lips lingering on her skin.

Charles simply bowed, but it was *his* figure that Davina fixed her eyes on as he vanished into the dim, rainy night.

Her heart felt heavy as she thought of the fortnight that stretched ahead.

It would have felt heavier still could she foresee the terrible events that were to befall herself and the man she loved before that fortnight was out.

*

Howard parted from his brother and Aunt Sarah at the gates of Priory Park, he to ride east, they to travel west.

Charles rode beside his aunt's carriage all the way to her home, where he left her in the care of her doughty housekeeper. He then turned north. He would ride until two o'clock and stay at a hostelry near Lalham, where at dawn he would catch the London train.

There was little moon. A damp mist settled about him like a shroud.

His horse trod carefully, the sound of its hooves seeming muffled.

Davina, Davina. Her name fell again and again from his lips. He was painfully bewitched by her. It was agony to know that he could never have her, for he would not woo where he had no security to offer.

His mind was too full of Davina to be mindful of his own safety.

They came at him out of the mist, three or four masked men. The first Charles knew was when his horse shied and reared. The second was when a blow from a cudgel unseated him and he fell heavily from the saddle. He was struggling for his gun when another blow caught him on his temple.

He staggered to his feet, struck out in defence, but the blows fell now from all sides. They came until he sank to his knees and still they came.

He tasted mud and then all sensation vanished, leaving only darkness and the inexorable drip, drip of rain on his unconscious body.

"Davina" was the last word he uttered, the name seeming to rise and float like gossamer in the night air.

CHAPTER FOUR

Davina lay miserably in the dark, listening to a distant rumble of thunder.

Six days had elapsed since the departure of Lord Delverton for London.

Six days of interminable silence, during which she had not received so much as a single word from him.

At first, she had chided herself for her childish impatience. She had to allow Lord Delverton time to arrive at his desk, surely, before she could begin to expect a letter!

He must sharpen his pen, fill his inkwell, set out his paper, wait for inspiration. Once he had written to her, he must fold the letter, set his seal, send for his servant to take the letter to the post.

After five days of silence, however, she felt she had to face the truth.

Lord Delverton had forgotten her. The glitter of London had erased his promise to Davina from his mind.

She began to sink into a deep melancholy.

Her mood was not alleviated by the visits of Howard. She barely registered his attentions, the bouquets of sweet smelling flowers he brought, the chocolates ordered from the special store in Lalham. She only turned her full gaze on him when he mentioned Charles.

Howard noted this with a frown.

He did not know whether Charles had an interest in Davina, but it was obvious Davina had an interest in Charles. This must be sharply nipped in the bud! All was fair in love and war. He was as good a match for Davina Shelford as his brother.

Better, he believed, for he was not so serious and was far more experienced with the fairer sex. He was convinced it was only a matter of time before he won Davina's favour.

To hold Davina's attention, Howard began to talk more and more about his brother. Soon he was insinuating that Charles had an eye for the ladies and was easily infatuated. He almost felt a twinge of guilt when he saw Davina's eyes mist over, but he knew he must eradicate all yearning for Charles from her heart before he could begin his own courtship.

"My poor brother," he sighed, "cannot resist a pretty face. It is the reason he is not married, although he is thirty years old and should be thinking about producing a Delverton heir. In the six months he has been back from Africa, he has squandered all his money on the ladies. Scores of them."

Scores of them! These words now haunted Davina as she listened to the approaching storm.

Her face felt hot in the stifling room. She threw aside her bedclothes and lay there in her silken shift. Lightning lit up the window behind the curtains and the growling thunder was like a beast let loose in the skies.

She moaned as she imagined Lord Delverton at this very instant in someone's embrace. Someone else's embrace.

She had misconceived his character just as she had misconceived the character of Felix Boyer. She was a silly, naïve fool. She would never in a million years have guessed

50

Charles to be a philanderer, but if Howard did not know his brother, who did?

The window, that she had left on the latch, blew wide open. The storm seemed to rush into the room, catching Davina up in its wake and flinging her down again into an abyss of despair.

She felt helpless in its force and longed deeply for strong and capable arms to hold her steady.

Arms that she increasingly felt could never be those of Lord Delverton!

*

In a place not too far distant, but unknown to Davina, Charles stirred his head in the dark and groaned.

The thunder without seemed to roll and crash within his very skull. His eyelids were as heavy as lead and it was with effort that he opened them.

Where was he?

A fire glowing dully in a hearth was all he saw at first, but each flash of lightening revealed a little more of his surroundings. A three-legged stool, a low, wooden door, rafters under thatch, a thin blanket covering him on the bed in which he lay. A window, such as those found in the cottages of poor tenant farmers.

Rain drummed on the thatch above.

How had he come to be in such a place? He struggled to remember.

There had been hooves on a dark road, then figures looming out of the mist.

He frowned as he recalled harsh voices – blows – the taste of mud.

After that, all was as a dream. There had been the flickering light of a fire – this same fire that burned before him now, no doubt. A cool flannel on his brow, a phial held to his lips, a voice urging him to drink. A liquid that seemed to burn his tongue. Tossing and turning on this pallet that smelled of hay.

A tall figure with dark hair, floating in and out of his consciousness.

Another figure, almost grotesque, with a shock of white hair and maddened eyes. This latter creature cackled at his bedside or crouched before the fire rocking to and fro on her heels.

One vision swam before him that was a balm to his shattered mind.

A girl with violet eyes, gazing sweetly at him. Now as he thought on this ghostly image, a name came to him. Davina. "*Davina*", he murmured aloud, and the sudden stab in his heart told him that this beautiful creature had at some point been a source of pain as well as comfort.

Attempting to rise from the bed, he realised he was injured. His right arm was in a crude sling and his head swam as he sat up. Lifting his hand, he felt a bandage about his brow. He swung his legs to the floor and winced.

His joints were stiff and he needed all the will power he possessed to climb to his feet.

He staggered to the door and opened it, his eye drawn immediately to the blaze of logs in a wide hearth.

At the creak of the hinge, a figure at the fireside started up. A bowl of hot milk clattered to the floor, a flash of worsted cloth passed before his eye and the figure was gone, like a cat frightened from its corner.

Charles was alone again. Or so he thought.

There was the tinkle of bracelets from the shadows and a woman stepped into the firelight.

She was carrying a pewter plate on which lodged a hunk of bread. A scarlet shawl was draped about her shoulders. These details escaped Charles completely, however, for his breath had almost stopped in his throat at the sight of the woman's face.

She had proud, dark, Romany features. Ebony hair tumbled to her waist and her almond-shaped eyes were the colour of jet. Her lips were lustrous, glinting like red berries on a winter bough. Everything about her – the profusion of bracelets, the green embroidered petticoats, the gold hooped ear-rings – suggested a gypsy. Her bearing, however, was as haughty and regal as that of an Egyptian queen.

Her voice when she spoke was deep and assured.

"So, you have risen," she said.

Charles managed a slight bow. "Indeed, madam. But it seems I am at your mercy and perhaps even in your debt."

The woman's eyes flashed in such surprise at the word 'madam' that he dimly realised she had not often been treated with the usual social courtesies.

He waved a hand at the stool. "My – apologies. I scared away your guest."

"No matter. She will come again," replied the gypsy.

The next moment she was at his side as he swayed with sudden dizziness and groped for support. Grasping his elbow with her free hand, she guided him to the stool and helped him to sit.

"It is no surprise that you are so weak," she murmured with concern. "You have taken no food for many days."

Charles stared up at her. "How many days?"

"Six."

He digested this information in astonished silence. He felt too weak to ask the questions that were plaguing his mind. He leaned against the wall and watched in a daze while the gypsy crumbled the bread she was carrying into a pot that swung on a hook over the fire.

She stirred the bubbling contents for a moment and then ladled some out into a bowl that had been warming on the hearth.

"Take this," she commanded, handing him the bowl and a spoon.

Charles obeyed, but after only a few listless mouthfuls he put down the spoon.

"I cannot," he muttered.

"It is soup made with rabbit. It is not good?"

"It is very good. But – I do not feel hungry."

The gypsy came close and pressed a hand to his forehead. "That is because you still have a fever," she stated calmly.

As she drew her hand back, his attention was caught by a glint from her left hand. It came from a red stone set in a gold ring.

Something about it disturbed him, but he could not think what. The next moment he had forgotten the ring, as the gypsy took the spoon and bowl from his hands.

"Come," she said simply. "You must return to the bed I made for you. You must rest some more."

"Rest more? Impossible. I must – I must be gone."

The gypsy said nothing but a wry smile played about her lips as Charles rose unsteadily to his feet and took a few steps towards the cottage door. A moment later he buckled and sank insensibly to the ground.

The cottage door swung open and a gust of rain swept in. Out in the wet night, a wild haired figure cackled at the sight of the gypsy supporting Lord Delverton back to his bed of straw.

*

Concerned at the increasing listlessness and pallor of his daughter, Lord Shelford decided that what she needed was more fresh air and exercise.

Accordingly he had approached Howard Delverton for advice on purchasing a pony for Davina to ride.

"My own horses are rather too large and highly strung," explained Lord Shelford.

"I have the very fellow to help you!" said Howard. "Jed Barker. He knows a great deal about horse trading. He will find you a pretty and well behaved little animal."

The very day after the storm, Jed and Howard rode up the driveway to Priory Park together, Jed leading a high-stepping white mare on a halter.

Lord Shelford was delighted and called for Davina.

"There, now, Davina," he said. "I don't know what ails you, but a trot out on that little creature will surely lift your spirits."

Davina, concerned that her father was so worried about her, forced a smile. "Why, Papa, how thoughtful of you! She's – she's delightful."

"Why don't you try her out immediately?" suggested Howard. "I would gladly accompany you for the ride."

"I am not dressed for such an excursion," murmured Davina.

"Mr. Delverton will wait in the library until you have changed," urged her father. "And his man can wait here with the horses."

"Begging your pardon, Lord Shelford," broke in Jed darkly. "I am not a servant."

There was an uncomfortable pause. Then Lord Shelford gave a bow.

"My apologies," he said. "You are of course welcome to join – Mr. Delverton and myself for refreshment."

Davina, embarrassed for her father, thought no more of resisting his blandishments that she ride out. She hurried to her room, where Jess helped her into her riding habit.

"He's a handsome one, he is!" said Jess as she adjusted the veil on Davina's hat.

"Whom do you mean?" asked Davina abstractedly.

"Why, that Master Howard," replied Jess.

"Oh," said Davina. "I suppose he is."

"*Suppose*, miss? Why, there isn't a young lady from here to Lalham wouldn't give their best bonnet to be in your place today, riding out with him."

"Would they feel the same if it was – his brother?"

"Oh, he's far too serious!" laughed Jess. "A girl wants someone who's ready for a laugh and a dance."

She could not read Davina's sad expression through her grey veil.

When Davina presented herself downstairs, Howard rose in delight.

"Upon my word, what an elegant figure you cut, madam."

Lord Shelford looked taken aback at this rather forward remark, but had to admit that he agreed.

"Very like her dear mother," he said fondly.

Jed drained his glass of whiskey and wiped his mouth on the back of his hand, saying nothing.

It was a fresh morning after the torrent of the night. The grass smelled sweet and damp and the hedgerows still glistened with beads of rain.

"What will you call your pony, Miss Davina?" asked Howard, trotting at her side.

"I haven't thought," replied Davina. "She is – very pretty. Such a dazzling white."

56

"Call her Gypsy, why don't you," growled Jed from behind. Howard gave an awkward laugh.

Davina glanced backwards. She was uncomfortable at the presence of Jed and wished Howard had sent him back to Lark House rather than have him ride with them. Jed made her think of a brooding animal – a dangerous animal, that lurked in forests, in shadows.

She was confused by his ambivalence towards her. One minute he regarded her with seeming contempt, another he flashed her a look of cold-eyed appraisal. She had the curious sensation of being somehow in his sights, like a forest creature that he surveyed down the barrel of his gun.

Shaking off these morbid thoughts, she patted her mount's white neck.

"I think I will call her Blanche," she decided.

"That's a pertinent name," smiled Howard. "We had a racehorse once called Blanche."

"You mean – your brother and you?"

Howard exploded with laughter. "I mean Jed and me. Charles buy a racehorse? He's more likely to buy a *cart*horse. It's all work for Charles."

Davina's brow creased. "But you said he spent all his money – on the ladies?"

"Ah, yes," responded Howard quickly. "Since he got back from Africa. It seems to have shaken him up out there. Hasn't it, Jed?"

"That's right," said Jed with a stifled snort.

Davina turned her head and was startled to see that Jed had urged his horse forward and was now riding abreast of her, on her right. With Howard on her left, she suddenly felt hedged in.

"Indeed," continued Jed, "I heard Charles got hisself somewhat involved out there. With the daughter of a local chieftain. If he hadn't left when he did, he might have woken up with his throat cut."

Davina closed her eyes in horror.

"Jed!" called Howard sharply. "Can't you see you're upsetting the young lady? Why don't you ride on to the smithy's and see if he's finished shoeing the carriage horse?"

Jed dug his heels so deeply into his steed's flanks that it reared up with pain. "As you wish, Delverton!" he leered, and spinning his horse round, set off at a gallop across the heath.

"Was that true?" asked Davina in a low voice. "About – Africa?"

Howard was silent for a moment. "My brother is a – an enigma," he said at last, in a somewhat uneasy tone.

'It must be true, if he does not wish to discuss it,' thought Davina miserably.

The more she learned of Lord Delverton, the more she realised that her image of him had been a chimera.

Would she ever learn to see a man as he truly was and not turn him into a figure of romance and fantasy?

*

Charles had relapsed into a feverish state of semi-consciousness. He had perhaps risen too soon and thus set back his recovery. He was aware of the gypsy once again tending him, bringing him strong smelling potions, placing dampened flannels on his body to cool him, changing the dressing around his brow. Finally she removed it altogether and it was at that moment that Charles opened his eyes to gaze at her.

"Your name? What is your name?" he murmured.

"Esmé."

"Esmé. Esmé," he repeated. "Is that all?"

"That is all."

Esmé made to turn away, but Charles caught at her hand and raised it to his lips.

"Whoever you are," he muttered, "you will always have the gratitude of the Delverton family."

To his surprise, Esmé drew back her hand as if she had been stung.

Charles's arm dropped to his side. "W-what is the matter?" he asked weakly, his eyes half closed.

"Nothing." Esmé, biting her lip, turned away and moved to the door.

"Sleep," she called over her shoulder. "Sleep will heal you. Sleep."

The door closed behind her.

How much longer he did indeed sleep Charles had no way of knowing, but the hour came when at last his mind felt clear and he was once again master of his thoughts.

It was a bright morning. Birds were singing in the eaves of the thatch and a ribbon of sunlight lay across the beaten earth floor.

Into the recovered clarity of his mind came rushing memories of the recent past. The death of his father – problems with the estate – altercations with Howard – Aunt Sarah's machinations – the ride to Lalham so cruelly interrupted by the attack. All of these memories were softened by the image of Davina, languishing in his arms after she had fainted.

For this alone, he would have been glad to survive.

He ran his hand over his chin and grimaced ruefully. He had grown something of a beard. He wondered what he looked like after so many days out of the world!

He rose and made his way to the other room in the cottage.

Something was gently bubbling in the pot over the

fire. Peering in, he determined it was porridge. His pangs of hunger surprised him. He was most certainly on the mend, if not fully recovered.

"Good morning," came a voice from behind him.

Esmé stood in the open doorway, green boughs swaying beyond her. She carried two pitchers of water.

Charles bowed. "Good morning. I feel I must apologise for looking so – unkempt."

In response, Esmé crossed the floor and emptied the pitchers of water into a large tub standing on a stool.

"For you," she pointed. "Give me your shirt and breeches and I will wash them."

Charles hesitated. "This – sling."

Esmé approached and swiftly untied the sling from around his neck.

He gingerly straightened his arm and clenched his fingers. He realised with satisfaction that he would not need to put on the sling again.

"Your clothes," Esmé reminded him.

Still Charles hesitated. Esmé gave him a mocking smile, took down a cloak from a hook and tossed it to him. Then she turned her back while he removed his clothing and dropped it all into a bundle.

"I will take these to the stream," said Esmé, picking up the bundle. "When I return I will serve breakfast."

He plunged his hands into the cold water. He felt as if he was washing away the fever and confusion of the last few days.

He was sitting wrapped in the cloak when Esmé returned. He watched her drape his wet clothes over the bushes outside. Then she entered the cottage and ladled out the porridge.

"This is delicious," he marvelled.

Esmé said nothing. She ate quickly, her eyes always on him, as if he might escape her if she looked away.

Charles felt her searching gaze. "It is strange to be eating together like this," he said, "when you do not even know my name."

"But I do know your name."

"You do?" He was momentarily taken aback.

"You said it to me. When you were feverish. You are a – Delverton."

"Ah, yes. I remember. Well, I am indeed a Delverton. Charles, Lord Delverton."

"There are no Lords in the forest," replied Esmé in a flash.

He looked beyond her, to the green, peaceful world visible through the open door. The sight of his breeches and shirt undulating on the swaying boughs made him smile.

"You are right," he said. "There are certainly no Lords in the forest."

He put his bowl down and gazed at his companion. "You are always alone here, Esmé?"

"Yes."

"You are never with – your people?"

A shadow crossed Esmé's brow. "No."

Charles mused for a moment. "So when did you come here?"

Esmé raised her large jet black eyes and spoke with complete frankness, "Two months ago. I was without a home. I found this cottage.

"It was empty and neglected and I made it my own. But it seems another considered it hers, for I returned one day to find a half mad creature – the woman you frightened from the hearth – sleeping in a corner. She never cared that I was here too and comes and goes as she wishes."

Charles nodded. "Well, it is lucky for me that you *were* here. How did I find you?"

"You did not. I found you."

He looked surprised. "You found *me*? I imagined that I was – injured in an attack and somehow stumbled to your door."

"You were attacked, but some miles from here. I was out hunting – "

'*For which read poaching,*' thought Charles, but he was not about to say anything.

"– and heard cries," continued Esmé. "I crept through the trees to see what was happening. Four or five masked men were beating you. I cried out and came forward with my knife and they all ran away."

"Your knife?" exclaimed Charles.

"Of course. I use it for hunting."

"You are very brave," he declared. "Those men had pistols."

"I knew they were cowards," said Esmé scornfully. "When I saw you, I thought they had killed you, but I felt your heart and it was beating. I brought you here on your horse."

"My horse?" he broke in delightedly. "You have my horse?"

"Yes. It is in a nearby clearing. The robbers took everything else and so I had no idea of who you were."

Charles was silent for a moment. "I owe you my life," he said at last. "How can I ever repay you?"

A strange look came into Esme's eyes. "I have saved you for your family. That is enough," she replied. Before he could respond she sprang to her feet. "Come. Let us go and find your horse. He will be glad to see you."

"Like this?" he exclaimed, indicating his beard and

the cloak in which he was dressed. "I look like a monk!"

"Your horse will not care," laughed Esmé. "And who else is there to see you?" She moved quickly to the door and looked enticingly back at him.

"Come!"

His horse, Faro, raised his head from the grass and neighed when they approached.

"He looks beautifully groomed," Charles remarked in surprise.

"I have looked after many horses," proclaimed Esmé proudly. "We were a circus family."

There was such a look of longing on her face that he knew at once how he could repay her for saving him. He said nothing for the moment, however, only asking her if she had ridden Faro. She confessed she had. Indeed, she had been 'practising' her act on him. Charles was intrigued.

"Show me!" he urged.

Esmé needed no further encouragement. She leapt onto Faro and he immediately kicked his heels with delight and set out at a canter over the grass. In one clear move, she swung herself up to stand on his shining flanks.

As Faro circled the clearing, Esmé raised a leg and balanced with all the grace of a dancer on the other. Then she slid down again to a sitting position and grasping a handful of Faro's mane, slipped sideways until she was almost under the horse's body.

"Bravo! Bravo!" Charles applauded.

The sun glinting on the trees – the proud look in Faro's eye – Esmé's grace – her lustrous dark hair flying out behind her – the birds wheeling over his head – all this gave him a sense of freedom that he had rarely, if ever, experienced.

He almost wished he could remain here forever, where there were neither duties nor cares to burden him. Remain here with this unhindered spirit, Esmé. Leave Lark House to the ministrations, inept though they would be, of his brother Howard. What did status matter, when there was this? The sweet, exhilarating rush of liberty?

Yet even as these thoughts swept him, a vision of Davina rose to his mind. Alluring though Esmé's dark eyes might be, they could not compare to violet – the rich ebony of her hair could not efface the memory of gold.

Of one thing he was now certain. This episode in the forest had taught him something. Life – and happiness – were to be grasped with both hands.

If status did not matter, then neither did pride. He would woo Davina, though he had little to offer her but his heart. He would woo her and make her his own.

Faro galloped towards his master and in one leap Esmé was at his side again.

"You admire me?" she panted.

Charles laughed. "I do admire you, Esmé. You are very skilful."

"It is in my blood," she replied simply.

The two of them started walking back to the cottage. Charles explained that he must soon return to his home, that afternoon if possible. Although his family and friends happened to believe he was in London, they must wonder why they had heard no word from him.

He glanced sideways at his companion.

"There is one thing I should like to ask you, Esmé."

"Yes?"

"I understand that at first you could not send to my house because my identity was unknown to you. But once I had divulged my name – it surely would not have been difficult to send for my family and enlighten them as to my whereabouts?"

Esmé bit her lip and looked away. "It is many miles to your house. I could not leave you alone for long. I had to make many potions from the herbs I picked. You must not ask me, anyway," she ended with such sudden and inexplicable anger that he thought it politic to probe no further.

By noon, his clothes were dry. Esmé, whose good humour was as easily restored as lost, insisted on shaving off his beard with her knife.

"You must not frighten your friends," she laughed. At last she stepped back and regarded him contentedly. "There. You are a Lord again. Now you cannot stay in my forest."

"I am banished?" he smiled.

He was astonished at the anguished look that crossed Esmé's face.

"Banished," she murmured. "Yes. Banished."

She accompanied Charles to the clearing where he saddled Faro in silence. He tightened the girth and then swung himself into the stirrups.

"Esmé," he said, looking down at her, "I am forever at your command."

"At my command?"

"Yes."

"Then there is one thing I command you. Tell no one about me."

He inclined his head. "If that is what you wish."

"It is."

With that, Esmé was gone, vanishing through the trees.

Charles looked after her for a moment and then he and Faro set off in the opposite direction.

The road through the woods was dark but he knew his way lay south.

South to home and to one whom he hoped would be

the joy of his heart.

*

Davina stood at her dressing table. Her sad, pale face looked back at her from the mirror.

"YOU DO NOT LOVE LORD DELVERTON, YOU DO NOT LOVE LORD DELVERTON" she told her reflection, but the sad expression in the glass did not change.

Something must happen, she cried in desperation. Something must happen to stop me thinking about him.

Quitting her room, she wandered the echoing house. In the gallery that ran along the front of the house, she walked to the window and leaned her face against the glass.

The driveway stretched out ahead of her. At its far end, a figure on horseback came into view. She struggled to control the sudden surge in her blood. The figure might be Lord Delverton – it might not – what did it matter either way? He could not fool her again. She knew now what manner of man he was.

Yet her heart would not be silenced.

The figure drew near. A black horse, an upright figure.

Davina breathed against the glass.

I will marry you, she suddenly decided. Whoever you are, riding towards me, I will marry you. Let fate decide in whose arms I lie.

"*I will be yours to eternity, whoever you are.*"

CHAPTER FIVE

The woods were dense around Esmé's cottage and Charles's progress was slow. Now and then a bird called from a low bough, or a squirrel pattered up the bark of a tree. Faro pricked up his ears at these sounds but otherwise plodded on with his head down.

He marvelled that Esmé was unafraid to live alone amid such silence.

He crossed a stream and found a rough track on the other side. This seemed at last a contact with that outside world from which he felt he had been in exile.

He wondered whether he would ever have left the un-hurried life of the forest had it not been for the memory of Davina. The call of duty was strong, but so was the call of paradise. The call of love, however, was stronger than either.

The trees had thinned and dappled afternoon sunlight fell across his path. The pale, golden hue of the air made him think of Davina – the curls on her forehead, the tresses that fell about her white neck.

Faro tossed his mane and quickened his pace, as if in answer to the sudden urgency in his master's blood.

Horse and rider moved as one, travelling eagerly now towards home.

The sound of a shot ringing out nearby brought Faro to a sudden halt.

He half reared and Charles ducked quickly to avoid the low boughs.

Swearing quietly to himself, he straightened in the saddle and peered ahead.

A moment later the figure of a man emerged from the trees, a bloodied rabbit swinging in his grasp. The man froze in his tracks at the sight of horse and rider on the path. Charles raised an eyebrow when he recognised the figure.

"Good day, Jed," he said coolly.

Jed, dumb-struck for a second only, spat out a wad of tobacco.

"And if it ain't Lord Delverton," he grunted. "You've kept yerself – quiet this last fortnight. No letters nor nothing. Your aunt was starting to fret."

"She is well, I hope?"

"Aye. Well enough." Jed plucked a string of tobacco from his lip, keenly watching Charles all the while.

"And my brother?"

"He's kept hisself – occupied."

Charles wondered if this meant that Howard had been gambling again, but decided not to pursue the matter for the moment. He gestured towards the rabbit carcass.

"I trust it is my land you are shooting on?"

Jed gave him a curious look. "Your land? We're a good few miles off your land here. Don't you know where you are, then?"

"No, Jed, I don't," he replied simply. "But I am, I hope, on my way home?"

"More nor less." Jed spat again. "I'll go on with you and show you the way. My business is done for now."

"Your business?"

Jed gave a short laugh. "That's right. My business.

Putting food in the Delverton larder."

Charles could not but flinch at this, although he would have been well within his rights to reprimand Jed. He sat in silence while Jed fetched his horse, which was tethered nearby. Jed threw the rabbit into a sack that hung from the saddle and then mounted.

The track was narrow and Charles permitted Jed to ride in front. For one thing, Jed was the more acquainted with the route, knowing which fork to take whenever the path diverged. For another, he had long harboured an instinctive dislike of having Jed at his back.

"Been in London all this time, have you?" Jed asked over his shoulder.

Charles knew that the attack upon his person was an event that would be of concern to everybody and must therefore be recounted. There seemed no reason not to begin with Jed.

"I never reached London, Jed. The night I left Priory Park, after escorting my aunt to her door, I was attacked on the road."

Jed gave a low whistle. "Attacked and never reached London, eh? Did You – did you happen to see who it was?"

"Three or four men. They were masked, as I recall. I can only assume they were the robbers who have been plaguing the area. They left me for dead."

Jed twisted round in the saddle and regarded him narrowly.

"You're not dead, though, are you? Not even scratched, I'd say."

"I was badly injured, but – I was found and nursed back to health."

"Was you, then?" Jed gave a laugh and turned to face forward again.

"The luck of the devil, I'd say! And who was it found

you?"

Charles drew in his breath, remembering his promise to Esmé.

"A – woodsman's daughter."

"Oh, aye? Pretty, were she?"

"As plain as a loaf," replied Charles quickly.

Jed's insinuation alerted him. He had no desire to have Jed – and Howard, always hapless in his friend's wake – scouring the woods with a pretty girl as their prey. Esmé and her cottage were sacrosanct and he would do as much as he could to protect her privacy.

"You will hear all when I am back home," he continued, anxious to forestall any further questioning.

Jed merely shrugged and rode on.

Another forty minutes or so brought the two riders to the edge of the woods. To his astonishment, Charles recognised the view that opened up before him.

"Why, that's the lake of Priory Park!" he exclaimed.

"That's right," said Jed.

"So these are Shelford's woods?"

Jed shrugged. "Some of them, yes. But there's miles and miles of woods t'wixt here and back where we met. Who's to say who they all belong to?"

Jed was obviously eager to justify his evident poaching that morning. But Charles's thoughts were on other matters entirely. All this time he had been no more than an hour or so's ride from Davina. All this time he had been a fugitive in her own father's woods.

All this time, Esmé the gypsy had been the unwitting and unacknowledged tenant of Lord Shelford, sheltering in one of his cottages, feeding from his own land.

Poaching his deer and rabbits!

It was an irony that he could not for the moment fully

encompass.

"Which way do you propose to go now?" he asked Jed.

"We can skirt the lake and go east, but that's the longer route. It's quicker by the road."

"Which we can only reach by riding across Shelford's lawns?"

Jed nodded. "Aye."

"Then that is the way we will proceed," said Charles. "We can be sure that Lord Shelford will not protest."

It was not so much a desire to reach his own home sooner that he had decided to cross the Priory Park estate as the secret hope that he might encounter Davina en route.

She could be walking in the rose garden or strolling in the drive that led to the gates. His hunger to catch even a glimpse of her was his over-riding desire.

The two men rode around the southern tip of the lake and galloped towards the house. As they drew near Charles became aware of a figure seated on the terrace. Nearer still and the figure rose to watch their approach.

It was Lord Shelford, cigar in hand.

"Delverton!" he exclaimed. "Well, well. Just back from London, eh? This is most unexpected. We have all been wondering at your – silence."

Charles was too impatient for news of Davina to wish to plunge directly into an account of what had happened to him.

"I am afraid I was – unexpectedly detained – " he replied, his eyes flicking to the windows of the house in hopes of seeing Davina.

"Were you, indeed? Well, London is one long diversion, of course."

Charles's attention snapped back to Lord Shelford, stung by the implication that he had neglected to keep his

71

promise to Davina merely because he had been otherwise amused. Before he could respond, Lord Shelford turned and called towards the house.

"Parfitt!"

Parfitt appeared at the open French windows. "Sir?"

"More glasses, please!"

Charles now noticed champagne in ice standing on a low table. His heart suddenly lurched with misgiving.

"Champagne?" he enquired. "What is the – occasion?"

Lord Shelford drew on his cigar and blew out a plume of smoke.

"That, Lord Delverton, you will presently discover," he answered, in a voice unmistakably tinged with regret.

Charles dismounted slowly.

There were voices from within and two people burst out onto the terrace.

He stiffened as he recognised Howard and – Davina.

Seeing his brother, Howard stopped short and exclaimed aloud.

"Charles! Dear fellow!"

There was constraint in his voice but he barely noticed. His eyes were on Davina, who had turned unaccountably pale at the sight of him.

"Madam," he bowed.

Davina did not curtsy in return, but began twisting a handkerchief in her fingers. Charles recognised it as the very one he himself had given her on the day he had called at Priory Park and found her indisposed. Sensing his stare, she blushed, and tucked the handkerchief quickly in her sleeve.

Howard's eyes narrowed.

"You have been gone a devilish long time, Charles,"

he said brusquely. "What kept you away?"

Charles was saved from making what must have been a lengthy reply by Parfitt, who appeared carrying a tray of extra glasses. The group on the terrace watched in silence as Parfitt made his way to the table. Jed meanwhile dismounted and stood with one foot resting on the lowest of the terrace steps, watching the proceedings from under his thick, black brows.

The pop of the cork sounded like the report of a gun in the strange silence that had overcome the company. As Parfitt filled the glasses, Howard leaned forward and took one from the tray.

"Here you are, Davina," he said, turning.

Charles started. *Davina.* He wondered at hearing this sweet name, the name that he had uttered so often to himself, spoken aloud in such an intimate fashion by his brother.

Everyone now held a drink.

"And what is the toast to be?" came Jed's dark voice.

Lord Shelford glanced at Jed with distaste. "I think it is for Howard to enlighten us on that subject."

Howard grinned uneasily. "That's right. And the first thing I have to tell you is – I am delighted that you are all here – and particularly delighted, Charles, that *you* are here. Yes. The truth is, you could not have arrived back at a more auspicious moment."

There was a pause. Charles tried to still his racing heart as he looked at his brother. "Indeed?"

"Indeed, old fellow. You can be the first to congratulate us."

Charles's eyes flickered to the waters of the lake, where a swan glided mournfully through the reeds.

"Congratulate you?"

"What! You can't guess?"

Howard caught at Davina's hand and drew her towards him. She stood, eyes lowered, trembling at his side.

"This morning I asked Miss Shelford for her hand in marriage and – divine creature that she is – she said yes. Do you hear, brother? Miss Davina Shelford is to be my wife!"

*

The drawing room at Priory Park was quiet. Davina sat in one of the window embrasures, her hands in her lap. With neither book nor embroidery to absorb her, her attention was focused on her father, who stood with his back to the blazing fire.

As the grandfather clock in the hall chimed the hour of seven, Lord Shelford took his gold watch from his waistcoat pocket and peered at it closely. Satisfied, he returned it to his pocket and stood waiting with his hands clasped behind his back. He was soon rewarded by the sound of wheels approaching the house.

The local gentry had elected to come to Priory Park that evening to discuss the recent spate of robberies in the area. No one felt safe, particularly after the most recent attack on Lord Delverton.

Lord Shelford did not learn of the attack until two days after Charles's return. It had not been alluded to that day on the terrace. Lord Shelford surmised that this was because he had considered it too indelicate a matter for the occasion.

Once he heard about the attack, Lord Shelford was deeply ashamed of his uncharitable suspicions regarding Charles's character. He really should not have made that remark about London being one long diversion.

He had been thinking that if Charles had not gone away – or if he had written as he had promised – Davina would not have been swayed by the charms of the younger brother.

He had been astonished when she professed her desire

to accept Howard's proposal of marriage. He could have sworn she was more partial to the elder brother but, he supposed, that was young women for you!

He had written immediately to Lark House to express his outrage at the incident and to offer any assistance required in apprehending the culprits.

It was generally agreed that some action had to be taken.

Davina listened as the doorbell sounded. Even as the door was opened more carriages were heard bowling up the drive.

Sir Vincent Clough was shown into the drawing room. He was soon followed by Lord Montley, Lord and Lady Criston, the Reverend Gee and a number of other gentlemen and their wives from the surrounding countryside.

Everyone settled themselves on various sofas, chairs and chaises-longues arranged for the purpose. Drinks were served and canapés brought in. The fire was merrily aflame and anyone coming upon the scene might well have imagined it was a lively social gathering, were it not for the grim expressions on many faces.

Davina remained apart, almost unseen in the unlit embrasure.

Aunt Sarah hurried in, looking somewhat flushed. Although her nephews had ridden alongside her coach, she had insisted on carrying her father's sabre with her for fear of being waylaid. She had barely allowed Parfitt to divest her of it in the hall.

Following close on Aunt Sarah's heels came Charles and Howard.

Davina saw her father's brow crease imperceptibly at the sight of Howard.

She knew that her father had been puzzled and disappointed at her choice of bridegroom. She could guess at his opinion on the matter.

Charles was not only the superior character by far, but it was he who held the family title!

Sighing, her eyes followed Charles as he crossed swiftly to his seat.

Howard meanwhile paused, searching for Davina. Lord Shelford signalled that she sat at the window and Howard came over to greet her.

Discovering after a moment that she refused to be drawn from her discreet corner, he kissed her hand quickly and rejoined his brother.

The drawing room door creaked open and a familiar figure slid through.

Jed did not attempt to join the rest of the company, but positioned himself at the back of the room, leaning against the wall with his arms crossed.

Davina had not set eyes on Jed since the day of her betrothal and the gathering on the terrace.

His had been the first and strangest response to Howard's announcement.

"God gives to those who have, eh?" he had said with a sneer. He had quaffed his champagne in one go, then leapt onto his horse and dug his heels so hard into its flanks that it whinnied in pain as it took off.

There had been a stunned silence broken only by Charles's steady voice.

"Felicitations, brother!" he had said, his glass raised. "And to my – sister-to-be. Felicitations."

Glasses had clinked but the champagne might as well have been ditch water for all the levity it produced.

Charles had soon bowed stiffly and offered his apologies. He must ride home and, on his way, would convey the – happy news to Aunt Sarah.

Since that day Charles had sought not a single second of Davina's company. He rarely came to Priory Park and if he did happen to accompany his brother and aunt on a visit, he placed as great a distance between himself and Davina as was permitted by the laws of common courtesy. He would greet her coolly and pass on, to speak to no matter whom, as long as it were not she.

"I have offended your brother," she finally remarked miserably to Howard.

Howard guffawed. "What? Charles? Oh, his nose is out of joint. He probably had his eye on some other match for me, that's all."

Davina began to wonder if Charles considered Shelford blood not elevated enough for the aristocratic Delvertons.

'He must have harboured that opinion all the time,' she thought sadly, 'even when he seemed to look on me with some favour.'

Seeing her so downcast, Howard attempted to reassure his fiancée.

"Charles has a talent for cutting himself off from a person when he wants. He'll come round. Besides, this recent adventure he has had – he's not been himself since, you know."

Davina was silent.

When the story of the attack on Charles had first reached her ears, she had been mortified.

How quickly she had rushed to condemn him for not writing to her as promised! She had never once considered that he might actually be *prevented* from putting pen to paper.

During the days that followed, however, she had begun to wonder about this 'woodsman's daughter' who had rescued and tended the injured Lord Delverton, particularly after she caught Howard winking at Jed and commenting on 'Charles's pretty nurse'.

Jed had merely grunted in return but Davina was transfixed.

She knew that Howard had no idea if the woodsman's daughter was pretty or not, but she could not forget his remark.

She tried desperately to convince herself that she no longer wanted Lord Delverton, but it was *he* who filled her daydreams, not Howard. It was *he* she longed to see and hear, not her fiancé.

The idea that a stronger motive than his injury had kept him lingering in the woods began to torment her.

She wished she had a greater command of herself than to attend this meeting tonight simply to see him, but such command she had not. That her fiancé was also present made her feel even more ashamed of her lack of character.

To any observer her gaze around the room may have seemed aimless, but it was no accident that it returned again and again to Lord Delverton's seated figure.

He was listening, head bent, to his brother Howard, who appeared to be talking with some urgency. There was an excited flush to Howard's features and his lips moved with unusual rapidity.

In contrast, Lord Delverton looked cool and remote, his hooded eyelids drawn down over his black, piercing eyes.

"Ahem!"

Lord Shelford coughed loudly and rapped his empty sherry glass. When he was sure he had everyone's attention, he set the glass on the mantel behind him and began.

"We are all gathered together with a common concern. This neighbourhood, once considered so safe – as many of you have assured me – has recently become infested with a species of parasite we all considered eradicated from our society. I mean, of course, the highway robber."

"It is not just on the highways they operate," broke in Sir Vincent. "I was within my own gates when I was attacked."

A murmur of alarm ran through the crowd.

"Nabbed me fob watch and me silver snuff box!" continued Sir Vincent. "Took me wife's silver pineapple brooch – she's still too shaken by it all to leave the house."

"Stole my whip and saddle," Lord Montley shook his head. "Though my horse bolted from them."

"And I was divested of my pearl buttons," wailed Lady Criston. "The ruffians sliced them straight off with a carving knife!"

Aunt Sarah's eyes had widened. "I will tell you who likes buttons," she ventured. "Gypsies, that's who. They simply adore such trinkets."

"I would hardly have described my buttons as trinkets," sniffed Lady Criston.

Aunt Sarah looked abashed. "No – no, of course not." She looked round helplessly. "But they're shiny, do you see. And gypsies wear shiny things."

"I do not think such remarks are very helpful, aunt," said Charles in a low voice.

"No, but the good lady has a point," boomed Lord Criston. "The trouble started soon after that tribe moved into Ledger's field, did it not?"

"It did!" agreed a number of voices.

Charles frowned. "That is merely circumstantial," he asserted.

"Circum – whatever – is enough for me," replied Lord Criston.

Lord Shelford, who had been listening intently, raised a hand. "I do not see where all this is getting us. We have to find out who the perpetrators are and then act swiftly."

"The gypsies! They are the perpetrators!" muttered Sir Vincent. "Look to them!"

The chorus of voices rose again, loud and angry. Davina thought it sounded like rooks cawing noisily in the trees. She wanted to put her hand over her ears.

"There's nothing wrong with – with gypsies," cried out Howard.

Davina saw to her surprise that he was biting his thumb anxiously.

Nobody heeded him. The Reverend Gee interposed a faint comment about 'charitable views' and 'Christian values', but no-one heeded him either.

"Why don't we raid the gypsy camp?" roared Sir Vincent. "And see what we turn up. If they haven't got *our* booty, they will have somebody else's, mark my words."

"Hear hear. Hear hear."

Amid the cacophony Charles rose, wine glass in hand, his brow creased angrily.

"You propose to raid the camp of possibly innocent people," he bellowed, "stirring up the men, frightening the women and the children and to what end? When you have your proof, then you might follow this course. Otherwise it is acting in a manner as uncivilised as the thieves that plague us."

"All that time in Africa has made you too tolerant of inferior creatures," remarked Lady Criston icily.

Charles's eyes flashed. "I have never, neither in Africa nor here, met with what you term inferior creatures," he snapped.

The Reverend Gee gave a mild nod of approval but

remained silent.

"What is this sudden concern for these gypsies anyway?" sneered Lord Montley. "Anyone would think you knew something more than we do about them."

"My concern is a simple matter of principle," replied Charles.

"Principle?" came a voice from the back of the room. "Or personal interest?"

Everyone looked round to where Jed leaned nonchalantly against the wall.

Charles's eyes narrowed. "What do you mean, Jed?" he asked.

Jed broke into a whistle that soon evolved into a tune. A tune that Davina recognised immediately.

'*My mother says that I never should*
Play with the gypsies in the wood.'

Everyone was looking at each other, perplexed, and only Davina noticed the faint flush that rose in Charles's cheeks. To her surprise, he did not respond to Jed's gauntlet, but finished his wine in one abrupt draft, his eyes locked sharply on Jed over the rim of the glass.

"I don't know what that fellow's insinuating," remarked Lord Criston "but I have to say, Delverton, you are the first landowner I've met who has any time for gypsies. They're as bad as locusts and it would be no harm to flush them out."

"I will take no part in any raid!" stated Charles firmly.

There was an unsettled pause. Despite the general high fervour, no one was anxious to undertake a raid without the support of the major landowner of the neighbourhood.

Lord Shelford spoke up thoughtfully. "Before we commit ourselves to hasty action, would it not be a good idea to send someone to reconnoitre the gypsy camp to see what can be found? After all, it could stir up more trouble than we've bargained for, if a raiding party sails in and then finds that the gypsies are indeed innocent."

"I doubt they are," muttered Sir Vincent, "but I'll grant you that to spy on them first is a sensible measure. Might catch one of them with my watch in his waistcoat."

"Trouble is," mused Lord Criston, "who do we send? And on what business? No one can just go nosing around the camp without a reason!"

Charles, twirling his empty glass in his hand, had been listening with growing interest. Now he spoke up slowly.

"I believe – I can solve that dilemma. I – may well have a legitimate reason to deal with the gypsies," he explained carefully. "All we have to do is find someone who could negotiate on my behalf. And I think I know the perfect intermediary."

"Who may that be?" asked Lady Criston eagerly.

Charles hesitated. "Jed Barker," he said at last, and his reluctance to admit that Jed might be of use was palpable.

Everyone looked hopefully at Jed. He stood tugging on his gold ear-ring. "It's true I've had some dealings with the gypsies in the past," he said.

"But there would have to be a good reason to send me along, Delverton. They're not fools, you know."

Charles regarded him coolly. "I am well aware that they're not fools, Jed. And have no fear, I do have a perfectly good reason for you to visit them, which I will discuss later. All I want to know is, do you accept the commission?"

Jed thought for a moment and then peeled himself away from the wall.

"I'll do it," he said. "Though I'm of your opinion, Delverton. I'll lay a wager they're not responsible."

They regarded each other unblinkingly for a moment and then Charles nodded. "Good. You and I will talk later."

His eye then swept the room. "Meanwhile, is everyone else agreed?"

Those present looked at each other before giving a general murmur of assent.

All this time, Davina had never taken her eyes from Charles's face.

His strange reaction to Jed's whistling a little while ago had taken her breath away.

My mother said that I never should

Play with the gypsies in the wood.

In the wood!

Davina's heart gave a lurch when she grasped what it was Jed had hinted at.

His 'pretty nurse' was not a woodsman's daughter at all. She was a gypsy, sure as Davina was a Shelford! And Charles cared so much for this gypsy that he had defended her people before all his neighbours.

Davina shrank against the window, her heart and mind in turmoil.

It was just as Howard had said. Charles could not resist the charms of any young woman he met.

'Not that *any* of it is my business,' Davina told herself fiercely. 'Lord Delverton is not my fiancé. Howard is.'

Yet even as she argued with herself, tears were welling in her eyes.

She did not love Howard. Her impulsive nature, her wilfulness, had led her onto this path that she suspected would lead to terrible unhappiness.

Yet she could not withdraw from the engagement. She could not bear for Charles to think even less of her than he already did.

83

She could not wound Howard, who had behaved with perfect – though sometimes strangely offhand – courtesy throughout. She could not admit to her father that she had made yet another romantic mistake.

Marriage to Howard was now her fate. *A fate she had woven for herself, a snare she had set for her own entrapment.*

The meeting was over and supper was announced. Howard came to Davina and offered his arm.

Behind him Charles was saying goodnight to Lord Shelford.

"You will not stay to supper?" Lord Shelford asked in surprise.

"Thank you, no, Lord Shelford. Jed and I have business to discuss."

His voice was cool, his back straight. Never once did he turn to acknowledge Davina's presence. Yet his neglect spoke volumes.

'You are nothing to me, Davina Shelford. You are nothing to me. I have no further interest in you.'

As Davina rose to her feet and took Howard's arm, a melée of words played mercilessly in her head.

My mother said that I never should

Play with the gypsies in the wood.

How could she ever have dreamed that this verse, sung to her by her mother so many years ago, would return to haunt her in such a cruel fashion?

CHAPTER SIX

Charles and Jed started along the drive that led to the park gates. Soon the lights of the house behind them disappeared amid the trees. Jed took out a piece of tobacco to chew and cast a sidelong look at Charles.

"So, Delverton?" he asked. "You have some business that'll take me to the gypsies at Ledger's field?"

Charles nodded. "Yes, Jed, I have. There is – something I want you to purchase for me."

"Oh, aye? And what might that be?"

"A horse."

Jed gave a grunt.

He might have guessed. Everyone knew that he horse-traded with the gypsies. No surprise, then, that Charles should think of him for this commission.

"Who's this horse for?" he asked.

"It is to be a gift for – the woodsman's daughter," Charles replied. "After all, she saved my life."

Jed moved the tobacco from one side of his mouth to the other. "You'll be looking for a carthorse, then?" he probed cunningly.

"No, Jed. I'll be looking for a thoroughbred."

Jed snorted. "Not much use to a woodsman's family!"

"Nevertheless," Charles retorted firmly, "a

thoroughbred is what I want."

"Well, then," declared Jed. "I'm your man. And you're right, it gives me the perfect excuse to take a look round the camp."

Three days later, Charles was retracing his steps through the woods to Esmé's cottage. He was riding Faro, but he was also leading a second horse, a sleek, grey mare with a black tail and a proud eye.

Now and then he glanced back at the mare with satisfaction. Whatever else one might say about Jed Barker, he was the best judge of horseflesh in the county.

Jed had bargained well with the gypsies and in the end the mare had cost considerably less than if Charles had purchased her from the local horse fair.

Jed had accepted gypsy hospitality once the deal was secured. He had plenty of time to look around the camp and he reported back that he had noticed nothing that might link the gypsies to the recent attacks.

Charles was relieved.

He was too fair a man to ever condemn a people out of hand, but now his concern was personal.

For the moment Esmé's people were safe.

Faro began to snort and toss his head and Charles surmised that they were near the clearing where the cottage stood. He could smell wood-smoke and soon he could hear Esmé herself, singing as she went about her chores.

He drew in the reins and swung down from his steed. Tying Faro and the mare to a tree, he proceeded on foot to the clearing.

He paused for a moment to take in the scene.

Esmé was kneeling at the stream that ran beside the cottage, scrubbing a scarlet petticoat on the stones. She was not alone. Watching her from the shade of the thatch –

crouched and rocking on her heels – was an old woman.

Charles remembered a figure starting up from the fireside when he first emerged from his sick bed and he remembered Esmé explaining about an old woman who often came to the cottage for shelter. This must be she.

The old woman suddenly spied him. She ceased her senseless rocking and watched him out of small, frightened eyes, but she did not flee.

Esmé looked up as Charles called her name. She rose to her feet in delight, the soaking garment still in her hand.

"You have come to visit Esmé!" she cried happily.

He bowed low and smiled. "I have come to visit Esmé, yes. I rode straight here from Lark House – "

It was as if he had cracked a whip or fired a pistol! The old woman gave a squawk, rose like a startled hen from her position, and took to her heels.

Charles stared after her. "I seem to have a most unfortunate effect on your companion," he remarked.

"It was the name of Lark House, it seemed to startle her," said Esmé. "Many curious things unsettle her." Esmé had come closer and was regarding him now with a frown on her countenance.

"What is it?" he teased, noticing her stare. "You do not like my cravat or my cape?"

"Oh," murmured Esmé with concern. "You are making jests, and your arm is not any more hurting, but your *heart* is hurting."

Charles drew in his breath. "Ah! Is my heart so visible?"

"To Esmé, yes," came the simple reply.

He regarded her for a moment and then smiled. "It is my pride that is hurting, no doubt, not my heart. But that is not a matter to dwell on now. I have brought you a present,

Esmé. Would you like to see it?"

"Yes," said Esmé.

"Wait there."

He returned to where he had left the horses. He patted Faro and untied the mare. She was a high-stepper and almost danced behind him as he led her out of the trees.

Esmé dropped the wet petticoat. She moved forward as if in a trance, until she was close enough to place a hand on the mare's neck. The mare whinnied and, lowering her head, nuzzled Esmé gently.

"She is mine?"

"She is yours."

"I shall call her – Lark," breathed Esmé, her hand on her heart. "Because you gave her to me and that is the name of your house."

Nothing would do but that Esmé should ride Lark straightaway and that Charles should accompany her on Faro. She leapt straight onto the mare's back and sat akimbo, her russet skirt falling to either side. She gave a whoop as they set off.

Just to the north of the cottage they broke from the trees and rode onto a wide, green plain, bordered a mile or so away by marsh. They galloped to the marsh and back, Esmé's hair flying in the breeze, her eyes ablaze with joy.

Laughing, breathless, they rode back into the clearing and dismounted.

"She runs well then?" came a voice from the direction of the cottage.

Jed lounged in the open doorway, a brace of pigeons at his feet, his shotgun propped against the jamb. The old woman had returned and was crouched nearby, humming under her breath. Charles noted that her eyes rested with uncharacteristic attention on the intruder.

It was the look on Jed's face, however, that most struck him. It was a look that suggested a sudden elevation of self esteem, though by what means, or on what pretext, Charles could not fathom.

Jed was tossing something in his palm, but his fist closed over the item as Charles advanced.

"What the devil are you doing here?" he asked.

Jed's eyes were suddenly like pools of black, brackish water. "I've had enough of you addressing me like a dog, Delverton. I'll thank you to address me as you would any gentleman."

Charles gritted his teeth. "When you behave like a gentleman, Barker, I shall be glad to oblige. For now, I desire you to answer my question."

Jed drew in his breath but seemed to decide that now was not the time to pursue this discussion. "If it's any of your business, which it ain't, I came to see *her*," he said coolly, jerking his head towards Esmé. "She and I, we're what you might call – old acquaintances."

Astounded, Charles turned to Esmé. "You – you know Jed?" he asked.

Esmé's eyes flashed. "I know him, but I do not like him," she replied fiercely.

Jed gave a grim laugh. "Oh, come now, that's not a pretty thing to say, when you haven't seen me for so long."

He turned to Charles, an ugly expression on his face. "I had a feeling she was in the woods and might be your – nursemaid. Is she to be your consolation too?"

"For what, pray?"

"Why, for your lady love marrying your brother instead of you."

There was a faint sound from Esmé. It was like the cry of a bird, deep in the wood at night. Charles barely heard it, yet he turned.

The blood had drained from Esme's face. Her eyes held a haunted quality as they fixed on Jed.

"That's right," nodded Jed at her with almost cruel satisfaction. "Miss Davina Shelford broke Delverton's heart. But he never had no right to her anywise, no more than has his brother. As I've only recently discovered."

Charles was taken aback at these words and was about to contest them when Jed spat a wad of tobacco onto the doorstep and held up his closed fist.

"By the by, *Esmé*, I found this on the stone by the stream. Very careless of you, my beauty."

Jed threw something to Esmé. An object that turned and turned and glinted like a red spark in the air.

Before it fell into Esmé's outstretched hands, Charles saw what it was.

A ruby ring.

Esmé clutched the ring to her breast and a sob rose from her throat.

Charles, concerned, made a move to go to her side, but she waved him away.

"No, please, go from here. Go," she choked.

Jed regarded Charles with grim satisfaction. "Marching orders, Delverton. I'll stay. She and I – we have some history to discuss. I have important information to impart, I have."

Charles hesitated. "Is this what you want?" he asked Esmé softly.

Esmé nodded wordlessly.

He mounted his steed with a heavy heart. He could not fathom the sudden turn of events, the depths of unhappiness Jed's words had engendered and the fact that nonetheless it was Jed who Esmé permitted to stay.

He rode away, Esmé's sobs ringing in his ear.

Was she weeping because she had discovered that he, Charles, loved another? It must be so and yet – what was the significance of the ring? What had Jed to do with it all? Why had he assumed a sudden air of malign confidence and what had he meant by those enigmatic words?

He never had no right to her anywise, no more than has his brother?

*

Later that afternoon, Aunt Sarah Delverton and Davina sat together in the drawing room at Priory Park.

Aunt Sarah insisted Davina call her aunt, since they would so soon be related by marriage. Her eyes filled with tears every time she looked at Davina.

Davina found the old lady somewhat absurd, but she was humbly grateful for the company.

Howard came often to Priory Park, but after kissing his fiancée's hand and enquiring after her health, he was as likely to disappear into the library to smoke with her father as stay to chat with her.

This afternoon Aunt Sarah had arrived and launched straight into a long dissertation on her own engagement – sadly brought to an abrupt end by the death of her fiancé in a hunting accident. Now and then she drew an enormous handkerchief from her reticule and blew her nose.

"We would have been very happy together, if he hadn't been gored to death," she sighed.

"What was the animal that killed him, exactly?" asked Davina politely.

"A wild boar," replied Aunt Sarah in disgust.

"Oh." Davina looked uncomfortable. "I do believe that's – what we're eating tonight."

Aunt Sarah patted her mouth with her handkerchief.

"Well. Never mind. It won't be the same one, will it?"

Davina was silent for a moment, her eyes on the fire.

"Will – Lord Delverton be coming too?" she ventured.

"If he is not too fatigued," sniffed Aunt Sarah, "after his woodland jaunt."

Davina tried to keep her voice steady. "W-woodland jaunt? What do you mean, Aunt Sarah?"

Aunt Sarah held up her spectacles to regard Davina. "Why, you've gone rather pink, my dear. Is it the fire? Shall I move the screen to your side?"

Davina shook her head. "No. I am really quite all right."

"Hmm." Aunt Sarah lowered her spectacles. "What was I saying? Oh, yes. The woodland jaunt. Well, you know that Jed was sent on a commission to the gypsy camp?"

"Yes. Has he returned?"

"Oh, yes, my dear! That's what your father and Howard are discussing in the library now. It seems Jed found nothing to suggest the gypsies have anything to do with all these horrid attacks. Well, I was always convinced of that.

"Anyway, he returned this morning, and Lord Delverton asked Howard to convey the information to your father. He could not come himself because he had – something to deliver that would not wait. And do you know what that 'something' was?"

Davina shook her head.

"A horse!" cried Aunt Sarah. "A horse, my dear. The purchase of it had been Jed's excuse for visiting the gypsies. No common cart horse, either. No. This had to be a thoroughbred."

Aunt Sarah pursed her lips in disapproval. "I ask you of what use is a thoroughbred to a woodsman's daughter?

The girl probably can't even ride!"

"It was for – the – woodsman's daughter?" asked Davina in a low voice.

"That's right. But I would have thought a sack of flour or a side of ham more appropriate."

Davina felt as if there was no breath in her body. *Lord Delverton had purchased a horse to give to the gypsy girl*! He must think a great deal of her indeed.

"Anyway, what must my nephew Charles do," continued Aunt Sarah, "but take immediately to the woods to deliver the creature. As if the woodsman's daughter couldn't wait."

'*It was Lord Delverton who couldn't wait,*' thought Davina miserably. 'Couldn't wait to see his gypsy again!'

The door opened and Lord Shelford appeared with Howard.

"Well, ladies," he announced, rubbing his hands together. "It seems we must look elsewhere for the answer to these robberies."

"I was always sure of that," said Howard. He sauntered to the sofa opposite Davina and flung himself into its depths.

"Well, I was not convinced either," admitted Lord Shelford. "And now of course with this latest occurrence – "

Aunt Sarah clutched at her breast in terror. "Another attack, Lord Shelford?"

"Yes," replied Lord Shelford, with an almost cheerful air. "In the early hours of yesterday morning. I have just told Howard the story. A gentleman, Squire Rutherford, was held up by four men on the road to Withyam.

"He tussled with them and managed to tear the mask from one of the assailant's faces. To his astonishment he recognised a stable hand who had been discharged from his service some weeks before."

"One of his own servants? But – what does this mean?" asked Aunt Sarah in bewilderment.

"It means, aunt," explained Howard, taking an apple from a bowl on the small table beside him and polishing it on his sleeve, "it means that the gypsies most certainly are not involved. They would never work with outsiders."

"It is most likely, therefore, to be an outfit of local men," said Lord Shelford. "Men who bear a grudge, men who are disaffected. But there has to be someone who's the brains of the operation. Finding him is the key."

"And – Squire Rutherford?" asked Aunt Sarah tremulously. "Is he – badly injured?"

"He was in great danger when they realised he had recognised one of them," said Lord Shelford. "Luckily, at that moment, one of the patrols we set up recently appeared on the road and the assailants all fled."

"It's a pity they weren't nearby when my poor brother was attacked!" remarked Howard. "It would have saved him the eventual expense of a horse." He took a bite of apple and leaned back contentedly.

"W-what sort of horse is it?" asked Davina.

"A grey mare," mumbled Howard, his mouth full of apple. "Pretty. A good trot on her. This woodsman's daughter must be a good looker."

Lord Shelford looked displeased at this casual mode of expression in front of his daughter. Davina meanwhile felt her eyes fill with tears and lowered her head quickly.

"I believe your brother delivered the horse today?" said Lord Shelford.

"He did," said Howard. "He came home at mid-day in a black mood. Couldn't get a word out of him."

He finished the apple and aimed the core at the

fireplace. It landed amid the coals with a hiss. Howard then leapt to his feet and stretched his arms.

"Think I'll take a ride before supper," he said.

There was a pause. Lord Shelford jutted out his jaw and stared into the fire. Davina kept her head lowered. Howard, sensing what was required, twitched his lips a moment and then held out his hand to Davina.

"Won't you – accompany me?" he asked. "We could ride round the lake together, if you like."

Davina had no desire to ride out with Howard. She wanted to retreat to the solitude of her room where her every blush would not be scrutinised by Aunt Sarah, her every expression not mulled over by her father. She knew that both of them were of the opinion that the engaged couple did not spend enough time in each other's company.

How could she explain to them that every minute spent with Howard further convinced her that she had made a terrible mistake? A mistake she could not rectify. A mistake she must nurse in her bosom and never disclose to anyone in the world.

Not looking up, she shook her head. "There are some letters that require my attention," she murmured.

"Well, then," said Howard, looking round at the company. "I shall return in an hour. Lord Shelford – Davina – Aunt Sarah." Howard bowed to all three and left the room.

Lord Shelford and Aunt Sarah regarded each other gravely. Before either of them could admonish Davina, however, she had risen quickly to her feet and was curtsying her excuses.

"I really – must retire," she insisted, and left the room.

"It doesn't look good, you know," came a voice from behind her as she made for the stairs. "You declining to ride out with me when I ask."

She turned. Howard stood there, drawing on his riding gloves. It was as if he had waited to accost her.

"I – can't help it. I want to be on my own," replied Davina.

Howard shrugged. He was not a cruel man and was often uncomfortable at the strategy he had pursued that had resulted in his undoubted prize. This beautiful creature, this heiress, who trembled in alarm at his most casual touch, paled at the faintest impress of his lips on hers. He had ceased to fool himself even slightly that she might be in love with him or even infatuated.

He could not begin to guess what had made her accept him but he was determined to be a good husband, when the time came. When the time came and he had her in his life and in his bed, he had no doubt he could change her emotional tune. No woman had ever withstood his amorous attentions for long. Meanwhile, he was not offended by her apparent lack of fervour. She was going to be his, along with her fortune. He could, for once, be patient.

"Well, as you wish," he said.

He watched her ascend the stairs. Her slender, graceful figure stirred him. He looked forward to his wedding night and to overcoming any – modest reluctance she might evince.

Yet even as his thoughts ran in this vein, his brow creased.

Another face, another love, another time, for a moment flooded his memory, struck like a dagger thrust swiftly under his heart. Then he shook himself.

'Howard, old fellow, let the past lie. Just count your – considerable fortune,' he told himself gaily, as he picked up his riding whip and went in search of his horse.

Davina meanwhile threw open the door of her room. She had come in search of sanctuary, but there was no sanctuary for her heart. It had no place to rest and no place to beat without pain.

She crossed the floor to her dressing room and stared up at the portrait of Evelyn Felk. The dark, troubled eyes gazed back and suddenly Davina remembered those words that Jess had spoken on first seeing the painting.

"That's asking for bad luck, that is, miss."

"It's you!" cried Davina wildly. "You are to blame."

She was hardly aware of her words, hardly aware of the irrationality behind them. Her distress flared to fury, her shame to blame. It was not she, Davina, who had brought herself to this pass. It was the malign influence of a woman who had lived and died thirty years earlier, a woman whose own love affair had not thrived and who had therefore put a curse on any passion that succeeded her in this house.

In this state of unreasoning rage, Davina dragged the portrait from the wall. Staggering to the window, she pushed open the casement.

She was going to eject Evelyn Felk from Priory Park and throw her to the air and the elements!

With the portrait teetering on the sill, Davina paused and squinted into the low afternoon sun. Slowly she lowered the painting to the floor and then leaned out to stare at the faraway woods.

Across the shimmering waters of the lake she spied a figure. Too distant to see clearly, she was yet aware of a cloak and wild, white hair blowing in the breeze. She was not sure whether she could actually make out these details or whether they had formed in her mind from a memory.

The memory of a face pressed against a window, wild eyes staring into the room where Lord Shelford and his guests dined.

She had the distinct impression that the figure was

watching the house, watching her, *willing* her towards itself.

It is the ghost, she suddenly shivered. *The ghost of Evelyn Felk*!

The ghost had materialised at the very moment she had been about to destroy the painting. She drew back from the window, her heart beating hard.

It seemed that the ghost had appeared to her, Davina, and no-one else. *As if it had business with her.*

This last thought decided her.

Ten minutes later, Lord Shelford glanced up in surprise as a figure on horseback galloped past the drawing room window. He supposed it was Howard and returned to his conversation about the forthcoming wedding with Aunt Sarah.

Davina urged her horse, Blanche, around the side of the house. Davina had put on her riding skirt and cape. Her veil fluttered as she rode.

She reached the farther side of the lake and turned along its southern shore. The wood lay to her right, intruding and receding by turn on her route.

Ahead of her, a figure turned at the sound of her approach. There was a glimpse of those wild eyes, hair streaming across a white, frightened face and then the figure vanished into the trees.

Davina drew on the reins. As her horse halted she fell forward onto its neck and lay there for a moment, panting. She smelt the leather of the bridle, Blanche's warm, rippling flesh beneath her hand. After a moment she raised her head.

Her ghost may have gone, but it had stayed until she arrived. It must be urging her to follow. It had vanished just at the point where a path ran into the woods.

Davina recognised the path as the one that led to Evelyn Felk's grave and her heart missed a beat.

What more proof did she need that her figure was the ghost of Evelyn Felk?

She peered into the darkening web of trees.

The low boughs and thick undergrowth decided her against taking Blanche with her. Though she would have dearly liked the company, she tied her to a tree and then set off through the trees, lifting her skirt high to avoid the roots that jutted across her route.

She trembled at every whisper of the leaves, every shake of a bough, yet still she stumbled on. She had come too far now. It was as if her quest would enable her to change the fate she had invited upon herself.

At last she thrust through the bushes to the clearing where the grave lay. Here, if anywhere, she expected to confront the ghost.

The clearing was deserted. Leaves rustled on all sides of her, birds settled in branches above her head, but there was no other sound, no other movement.

She did not know if she was disappointed or relieved. She moved nearer to the gravestone and gave a start.

The bunch of flowers that had been there was gone. In its place was another, fresher bunch, this time of wild iris.

Her ghost had come this way only a moment before. Yet of one thing she was certain. Ghosts do not pick flowers.

She was no nearer knowing the identity of the figure who, deliberately or not, had lured her to this spot.

She lifted her veil to brush strands of hair from her forehead and then froze.

Angry voices were approaching the clearing. Two men were quarrelling. She heard the name '*Esmé*' repeated once or twice and then, to her horror, there came the unmistakable sound of blows.

She turned around blindly, seeking the exit from the

clearing. She heard grunts, curses, the thud of fist on flesh.

The bushes before her parted and Howard staggered into view. His nose streamed blood and one of his eyes was half closed.

Davina gave a cry of horror. "W-what has happened?" she cried.

Howard stood swaying, shocked and furious to find her here, witness to this incident.

"This is – of no concern – to you. No concern to – a woman," he glowered and wiped his hand under his nose. "Get out of here. Go back to the house."

Davina backed away from him. When she felt the bushes behind her, she turned to push her way through to the path.

The last thing she saw as she glanced behind her was Howard, sinking to his knees in the clearing. Behind him, fist clenched, face a mask of fury, stood Jed Barker.

Esmé, Esmé, Esmé.

The name rang like a bell in Davina's ears as she stumbled along the path.

She knew in her heart who Esmé was.

Jed and Howard had been fighting over her. Lord Delverton was ensnared by her.

She was the gypsy in the wood and Davina was powerless before her charms.

CHAPTER SEVEN

The following morning Miss Regine Shelford and her fiancé, the Duke of Bedley, arrived from London. They were to attend the special supper planned in honour of Davina's engagement to Howard Delverton.

Lord Shelford met the Duke's coach at the door. He embraced his elder daughter warmly and shook the Duke's hand. Regine's chaperone, meanwhile, a lady of severe mien and ample bosom, descended from the coach and stood waiting with a grimly disapproving air.

Mrs. Crouch – for that was her name – had been employed by Lord Shelford in London and she had not expected her duties to bring her this far north. It might as well have been outer Mongolia, for all she knew of it!

Regine was looking round impatiently. "Papa, where is Davina? I thought she would be here to greet us!"

Lord Shelford's brow was troubled. "She is somewhat indisposed, my dear. She came in from a ride yesterday and has barely left her room since."

"If you will excuse me, Papa, I shall go to her at once," she said.

"By all means, do go and try to cheer her up!" said Lord Shelford. "I shall look after the Duke and – Mrs. Crouch."

Peeling off her travelling gloves, Regine hurried into

the hall and up the wide staircase to Davina's suite.

She found Davina sitting with one elbow on her dressing table, chin propped in her hand. Before her lay sheets of white paper, on which she seemed to be doodling.

"Davina?" she ventured.

Davina raised her eyes. "Oh, Regine. You have arrived."

Regine tried to ignore her sister's less than enthusiastic greeting. She bustled forward and, laying her gloves over the top of the mirror, began to remove her hatpin carefully.

"What a journey! Listening to that dreadful Mrs. Crouch and her complaints. I should like to have left her behind, but then I would have had to travel in a separate coach to the Duke, which wouldn't have been at all cosy. Although I was hardly able to enjoy much of his company, for the moment he is in motion, he falls asleep. He even falls asleep on horseback. Well, at least he was spared the worst of Mrs. Crouch."

All the while she was discoursing, in an apparently carefree manner, Regine was busy examining her sister's reflection in the mirror. Now her gaze dropped to the drawing paper and her eyes narrowed.

"What are all those faces, my dear?"

Davina stared down at the paper. "Those? Oh, they are – gypsies."

"Gypsies?" repeated Regine in amazement. She reached down and shifted the uppermost sheet towards her so that she could see it clearly. "All females, I see. And who is this – *Esmé*?"

"That's – the name. Of the gypsy."

"Oh, you're preparing a portrait? But the faces are all so different."

"Yes."

"It's not a portrait of a real person then? Well, silly me, why would it be? Where on earth would you have encountered a gypsy!"

"She – *is* a real person," replied Davina slowly. "I just – haven't ever seen her."

Regine stood poised with the hatpin in her hand.

"Then why, pray, are you attempting to draw her?"

"I – just want to know what she looks like."

Regine took off her hat and thrust the hatpin through it firmly. "Let me clarify. You are attempting to draw the face of a gypsy whom you have never seen, because you would like to know what she looks like?"

"Y-yes."

"My dear, you *are* a quirky goose! I do hope you will not display too much of this originality in the presence of my fiancé. I hope you will conduct yourself – *comme il faut* – when you meet him."

"I shan't mind if I don't meet him at all," said Davina truthfully. "I am not at all in the mood for company."

"Davina, what *is* the matter?" she asked at last in gentler tones than she had hitherto used.

Tears welled in Davina's eyes as she replied.

"I can't tell you. But if I knew – what she looked like – this Esmé – I think I would understand more."

Regine wondered what this obsession with Esmé signified.

"Davina," she said carefully. "Are you feeling at all doubtful about Howard Delverton's affections? Because it is not too late to withdraw from this engagement if there is anything – amiss. However, I must point out that this Esmé you are so concerned with is nothing more than a gypsy, while Howard is a gentleman. I am sure he would never have anything to do with – such a creature."

Davina listened with her head down. How could she explain that it was *Lord Delverton*'s involvement with Esmé that troubled her, not Howard's!

Indeed, she was no longer certain that Howard had anything at all to do with Esmé. It was *Jed* who had uttered the name of the gypsy during that – unseemly brawl yesterday in the wood.

And it was Jed who had taunted Lord Delverton about the 'gypsies in the wood'. Was it not conceivable that, encountering Howard by accident yesterday, Jed had proceeded to defame him, thereby prompting Howard to defend his brother's character?

"Davina?" frowned Regine.

Davina shook herself and looked up.

"It is not at all as you imagine," she said slowly. "It's just that I heard – Jed Barker – declare this gypsy to be more beautiful than any society lady could ever be. And Howard begged to differ. I think they have laid a wager of some sort and I – am afraid that Howard is going to lose."

She almost blushed to see her sister's frank gaze upon her. She had never told a lie to anyone, but she felt she could not possibly divulge the whole sorry truth.

Regine gave a chuckle of relief.

"And I suppose you are also worried that Howard will see this paragon of beauty and fall head over heels in love with her? Well, I have heard of this Jed from Papa. A savage, by all accounts. He could no more appreciate real beauty in a woman than he could appreciate bone china.

"I would lay *my* money on this Esmé having as red and rude a countenance as – as Mrs. Crouch. And if you're still worried about her, then I suggest you must somehow contrive to set eyes on her yourself.

"Now. Brush your hair and come down to meet my Duke. Thank heaven he is only interested in breeding cattle and barely notices women at all!"

Davina's brimming eyes widened. For a moment she forgot her own concerns. "But – but he surely notices *you*?"

Regine gave a hearty laugh. "Ah, yes, but you forget – I have the face of a heifer! Now, come along, little sister. No more moping!"

Rising from the edge of the bed, Regine took up a brush and handed it firmly to Davina. As Davina began to tidy her hair, her mind, like a sparrow to its nest, returned to the matter of Esmé.

She was too fair-minded and too romantic to console herself with the idea that no true gentleman could fall in love with a gypsy. However, if Esmé should indeed turn out to be – red and rude of countenance – then it would surely indicate such a weakness in Lord Delverton's character and such a lapse of taste and judgement, that she, Davina, might be released from her misery!

Lord Shelford was delighted when Davina came down to meet the Duke.

The Duke was charmed. 'Damn me if the gel didn't have the look of a newborn colt about her!' He insisted she sit by him at supper, where he spent the entire evening regaling her with advice on the various methods of breeding cattle. Davina listened with perfect, if subdued, composure.

No one present could tell that, as the Duke droned on over his sherry, one thought and one thought only consumed her.

How could she contrive to set eyes on Esmé, the mysterious gypsy in the Wood?

*

Next morning, a chill mist hung over Priory Park, wreathing the trees like cobwebs. The house itself was very quiet, save for the chink of scuttles as servants hurried to light the fires.

Lord Shelford, the Duke and Mrs. Crouch all snoozed still in their respective beds. Only Regine was up and about, having set herself the task of overseeing the preparations for the engagement supper that night.

Davina, in her green velvet dressing gown, sat alone in her room.

Tonight she would see Lord Delverton and more than anything in the world she wanted to look upon him with – with *contempt* rather than longing.

She had not slept well. All night images of Esmé had sifted through her mind, each one more outlandish than the last. Esmé had hair as coarse as marsh grass and eyes the colour of a puddle. She had fingers as thick as sausages. She had a wind-chaffed nose and skin like tanned leather. She looked like a butcher's wife, a fishwife, a laundry woman.

Only a man of debased tastes, such as those who frequented cockfights and low taverns, could be in love with her. If Lord Delverton was *that* kind of man then she, Davina, would be truly free!

There was a knock at the door and Jess appeared with a tray of tea and biscuits. Davina had decided that she did not want to go down to breakfast that morning.

"Jess."

"Yes, miss?"

"Are there any gypsies living in the wood?"

"In the wood, miss? No. I don't think so. They're all camped out on Ledger's field."

Jess placed a silver spoon on the saucer and handed the cup to Davina.

"There used to be lots of ordinary folks lived in the woods, of course," she continued. "Charcoal-burners and woodcutters. But gradually they drifted to town where work was more plentiful. So the cabins they lived in, which were only mud and thatch to begin with, just fell away. There's nowhere left for anyone to live in now. Biscuit, miss?'

Davina took one absently and laid it on her saucer.

"Though Martha's place might still be standing," mused Jess.

Davina looked up. "Martha?"

"Martha Tolman. Evelyn Felk's maid. She grew up in the forest. Her family lived there, though by the time Martha was working at Priory Park, they had gone to Laddleborough to work in the mill. Anyhows, their cottage was the only one built of stone, so it's more than likely still standing."

Davina put down her cup and stared at Jess. If the Tolman cottage was the only place left in the wood that a person might inhabit, then that was the likeliest place she would find Esmé.

"Do you know where this cottage is, Jess?"

Jess considered. "It's way over near the marshland, I believe. Why do you ask, miss?"

"Oh, just idle curiosity," murmured Davina. She crumbled the biscuit on her saucer thoughtfully.

Two hours later, Davina was trotting into the woods that bordered Priory Park.

Mist still hovered, wraith-like, between the trees. There was no sound in the woods, not even a birdcall. All Davina could hear was the soft thud of her horse's hooves on the mossy path. Her own heart seemed to beat in parallel time.

There was no other thought in her head than the urge to set eyes on Esmé, but no strategy as to how she would proceed once she found her.

She rode for a good while and then reined in. While Blanche drank at a stream she drew a paper from her sleeve and regarded it closely. She had spent the morning in her father's library, consulting various maps of the area until she found one where the woods were depicted in detail, complete with various paths leading to clearings.

One or two habitations were even marked and one in particular had drawn her eye. It lay in a clearing near that edge of the wood that bordered the marshland and there was a name printed beside it – *Tolman's cottage*.

She had hastily copied out the route to the cottage and now she studied it. She folded the paper and replaced it in her sleeve. Tugging on Blanche's reins, she urged her forward.

The sun was high in the heavens when the trees before Davina opened into a glade and she saw before her a stone cottage with a low thatch roof.

Davina's heart quickened. If this was Tolman's cottage, then it was not deserted. Somebody lived there and who else could it be but Esmé?

The cottage door was closed. She knocked and listened. There was no answer from within. Hardly aware of what she was doing, almost as if to escape the blood pounding in her temples, Davina slowly lifted the latch and stepped inside.

The interior was dim, the window being small and set deep in the wall.

She could however see that the floor was well swept and the small table well scrubbed. Two tin mugs stood on a shelf and a broom leaned upright in a corner.

She began to make out one or two more colourful items. A hand-painted candlestick stood on the mantel. A red enamel pitcher stood on the table. A purple and gold shawl lay idly thrown over the back of a crooked chair.

Hesitatingly, Davina picked up the shawl. It was of a soft weave and from it rose a faint scent of jasmine.

"Who are you? What are you doing here?" demanded

a voice from the doorway and Davina spun round in shock.

No butcher's wife or fishwife, no laundry woman with a rude, red countenance met her eye. Instead she saw a being as rare and exotic as – as a mountain orchid. In one miserable instant, she knew that this was Esmé.

No wonder Lord Delverton and Jed were so infatuated with her!

Esmé regarded her intruder imperiously.

"You cannot speak?" she asked haughtily.

"I am s-so sorry," began Davina, feeling herself tremble now that she was face to face with the woman she had so assiduously sought. "I did not mean to – trespass. I was hoping for – some water. I have been riding for some time." Her gaze fell as she saw Esmé's eyebrow rise. "I – lost my way," she ended limply.

Esmé walked past her to the shelf. She took down one of the two tin mugs and walked to the red pitcher that stood on the table. She poured and brought the mug to Davina.

"Water," she said.

Davina dropped the shawl and took the mug from Esmé who watched as she drank.

"You rode into the woods alone?" she asked.

"Y-yes."

"Where have you come from?"

"F-from Priory Park."

Davina sensed Esmé's sudden stillness and looked up at her, perplexed. She would have expected Esmé to react to the name of Lark House, where Lord Delverton lived, not Priory Park, where she, Davina, lived.

"Do you – know it?" she asked carefully.

Esmé's black pupils seemed to constrict. "I know it. I have heard – there is to be a wedding at Priory Park," she said.

"There is," admitted Davina in a low voice. "Mine."

It was humiliatingly obvious that Lord Delverton had discussed her and her affairs with this gypsy!

Esmé turned and regarded her.

"Why are you not happy?" she asked scornfully. "Do you not love the man you will marry?"

Davina drew in her breath, dismayed that Esmé could read her heart.

"I hardly think – that is a question a stranger should ask."

Esmé gave a sudden, fierce laugh.

"A stranger? You call me a stranger?"

Swiftly she moved across to Davina and stood, glittering eyes fixed on her face. "I am no stranger. We have much in common, you and I!"

'She knows,' thought Davina in alarm. 'She knows who I am and that I am drawn to Lord Delverton, for what else could we have in common but he?'

Esmé was so close that Davina could detect the heady scent of jasmine from her hair. She imagined Lord Delverton here, in her place, so near this paragon, this wild, forest creature. How could he resist such allure?

"Bah!" exclaimed Esmé, watching her closely. "Let us not pretend any longer. Your visit here is no accident. What is it you want from Esmé?"

Davina faltered.

"I w-want to know – how you f-feel."

"How I feel! I will tell you. Here." Esmé beat her breast vehemently, "here in my bosom lies a love that will never die. Never! But what can you know from that? You – you are too pale and spoilt for such passion."

At the word passion, Davina's eyes opened wide. Esmé drew back in surprise at their violet intensity.

110

"You know nothing about me!" Davina cried. "Only that I am to marry and that I – that I love the man *you* love."

Esmé paled. "So you do love him?"

The reply flew from Davina's lips unchecked.

"Yes. With all my heart. Yes." She felt faint at this admission, barely made to herself before now, let alone to another.

In one, unexpected move, Esmé pressed her hand over her face. "And *he* – does *he* love you?" she whispered.

Behind her long, splayed fingers, Esmé's flesh seemed drained of blood as she waited for the reply.

Davina stared. Was Esmé then so uncertain of Lord Delverton's affections? Had he behaved towards the gypsy as Howard intimated he behaved towards many women – inviting their affections and then withdrawing his? Was he really so cold and callous?

She hung her head as she spoke what she now perceived to be the truth.

"I do not think – he loves anybody," she said miserably.

"Can this be true?" moaned Esmé.

She raised her other hand to her face and Davina started as she saw the glint of her red, ruby ring. Her blood chilled. There was no other way the gypsy could acquire such a costly jewel, but that it was *given* to her.

Howard's words on the subject of his elder brother rang again in Davina's ears.

"In the six months he has been back from Africa, he has squandered all his money on the ladies."

Her courage was suddenly spent. She had learned more than she wished to learn, admitted more than she wished to admit. Even to herself.

"I-I must go," she murmured in distress.

111

"Wait!" Esme raised her face from her hands. Her features were drawn and her large eyes wet with tears. "It would be wrong – not to tell you – that there is danger for you – danger – "

Davina's hands flew to her ears. "You are trying to frighten me! I will not listen to you, I will not listen – "

Esme's expression changed in an instant. The tears in her eyes glittered now like splinters of ice.

"Go then, fool that you are. Go. But do not believe it is finished between us. His heart is mine. Whatever you say. His heart is *mine*."

Without a backward glance, Davina stumbled past Esmé to the door. The chill mist outside seemed to mingle with the tears on her cheeks.

She had only herself to blame but oh, how she wished she had not come within Esmé's orbit! Lord Delverton was now so low in her esteem that she did not know how she was going to bear his company that evening at supper, how she was going to bear his company as her brother-in-law in the months and years that stretched ahead.

Her mind teeming with such thoughts, she was well nigh at the copse where she had left her horse, before she realised that Blanche was not alone.

A man stood leaning against the tree to which the reins were tethered. It was Jed. His own horse, head low, was cropping roughly at the damp grass.

Davina hesitated and then walked forward slowly, blinking away her tears.

"Well, well, and what brings you so far from home, Miss Davina?" Jed asked with a leer.

Davina untethered Blanche before she replied.

"What brings me here is no business of yours, Jed Barker." She hoped she sounded calmer than she felt.

"Bin having your palm read by a gypsy, is my wager," smirked Jed. He watched Davina as she attempted to mount.

With his eyes on her, she lost her usual confidence and her foot slipped from the stirrup. Jed heaved himself away from the tree and, interlacing his fingers, offered her his hands as a step-up. She had no choice but to accept.

She felt herself lifted and in a second was perched sideways in her saddle. She extracted her whip from where she had thrust it through the bridle and only then did she meet Jed's eyes. Their intense glare unsettled her and she looked away.

"T-thank you," she said. She reached quickly for the reins and only then realised that Jed had kept a firm hold of them.

"W-would you let go, please!" she demanded, trying to keep her voice steady.

In answer, Jed twisted the reins more tightly round his fingers.

"Oh, I don't let what I catch go that easily!" he crowed. He whistled through his teeth for a moment, his eyes fixed on Davina. "So what did the fortune teller reveal about your future, eh?"

"Nothing. I did not come to have my fortune told," replied Davina.

"Nothing?" Jed looked surprised. He ran his tongue over his lower lip, clearing away some white flecks that had gathered there. "She plays her cards close," he muttered.

Davina was puzzled. Who was he talking about, herself, or Esmé?

The next moment she started as Jed laid his free hand on her foot.

"How – dare you!" she cried, trying to wrench her foot free.

"How dare I what? Touch your foot? I'll touch more than that if I so wish."

You – must be mad," she gasped.

"Mad?" Jed bared his teeth in what passed for a smile. "Oh, yes, that's more than likely. Mad for what is denied me, mad for what is mine by rights."

"You can't – you can't mean *me*?"

"You? Let's put it this way, my beauty. Having you would get me what's mine, to be sure."

"You forget yourself," said Davina desperately. "I am to be married, very soon now."

"I'd a-thought *she* would have changed your mind for you on that score," murmured Jed. "But if she hasn't, I can. When you hear what I've got to tell you, you'll turn to me, my beauty. And you've no idea what pleasure I can give you. Pleasure you can't imagine."

Desperately Davina tried to tear the reins from his grasp, tried to urge Blanche away, but Jed hung on tight. He pulled the horse's head lower and pressed his body against Davina's leg so that she felt herself pinned to the saddle.

Then, to her horror, he slid his hand under the hem of her skirt and began to caress her ankle. She struggled to kick him away again, but the weight of his body held her leg fast. In despair, she raised her whip. He barely flinched as the lash met his flesh. A thin line of blood appeared on his cheek and began to trickle into his mouth but he paid no heed.

"Oh, I did not mean – I did not mean – " Davina could not finish her words, for she did not know what it was she wanted to say. She had never hurt a human being in any way in her life and it shocked her. For a moment she was unable to move or think.

"Don't you worry none!" Jed muttered. "Hurts no more than the bite of a gnat."

"I-I'm sorry," whispered Davina again.

Jed released her ankle and wiped his mouth. He looked at the red smear that now lay on the back of his hand, turning it this way and that. Then he raised his burning gaze to Davina's face. It seemed to scorch her flesh, yet she was held fast by him, transfixed.

"What a thing to do," muttered Jed, "when all I wanted was to give you my treasures. Just look here, look here. Look at all the pretty things I have here for you. More than Howard Delverton could give you."

Davina gazed, mesmerised, as Jed drew back and plunged his hand into a pouch hidden beneath his greatcoat. Gold coins spilled through his fingers, jewels, watches. All tumbled into the ferns at his feet. Then he held a sparkling brooch out on his palm.

"Lean down, my lovely. Lean down."

His eyes, gleaming with unreason, intrigued her. His voice, low and coaxing as when he tamed foals, soothed her. In a daze, she slowly leaned from the saddle. He kept his gaze fixed on her as he drew aside her cloak and began to pin the brooch to her bosom.

"That's it, my pretty," he breathed. "You can trust me, you can trust Jed. Such treasures he has for you, for all his madness."

It was only the sharp prick from the brooch, as Jed manoeuvred it into place, that brought Davina to her senses. With a cry she pulled away. Blanche reared in fright at the sound and her right hoof caught Jed a blow on his temple. As he staggered back, Davina tugged hard on the reins, turning Blanche about. With a hard kick to her flanks, they were off.

Jed's roar of anger followed their flight.

"If I can't have you, no one shall. If I can't have what is rightly mine, no one shall. D'you hear? No-one!"

Davina flew careering through the woods. She did not dwell on Jed's parting words. The man was mad, pure and simple! All she wanted was to put distance between herself and him.

She had no idea if she was riding in the right direction. She trusted that Blanche would find the way. Mud flew from under the horse's hooves, spattering Davina's skirt, her hands, even her face, but she did not care. Home – home and safety was her only concern.

The sun was low in the sky by the time Blanche broke from the wood and, neck stretched taut, galloped around the lake and towards Priory Park.

Which way should she go? She did not wish to be questioned nor seen in her dishevelled state by her father or Regine. How could she tell them what had happened to her on a journey she should never have made?

She remembered a door on the kitchen side of the house that led into the passageway for the flower-room, the silver room and gun room. If she slipped into the house that way she might avoid encountering too many prying eyes.

She tried the handle. The door was locked. What was she to do now?

There was nothing for it but to slip around to the terrace and hope no one was in the drawing room at this hour.

She was shaking by the time she reached the terrace steps and anxiously scanned the windows for any sign of life. She did not notice the glow of a cigar in the dusk, did not see the figure sitting on the balustrade above.

She lifted her skirts and began to climb. Each step seemed the height of a mountain to her. Reaching the top, her fragile strength gave out. She sank down onto the cold stone and, palms to her face, burst into tears.

A hand grasped her elbow firmly and a voice

murmured into her ear.

"Hush now, hush. Let me help you up."

The voice was no balm to her. Its familiar tone struck her rather with fear and disgust. She tore herself free and scrambled unsteadily to her feet.

"Not you. Not you," she panted to an astounded Lord Delverton.

She swayed as she stood before him, her eyes full of anger. She might have stumbled on but that her legs began to buckle again. Charles threw his cigar to one side before he grasped her arm and held her firmly.

"Pardon me, madam, but you must accept my support. Whatever ails you, you do not seem strong enough to continue on alone."

"I do not wish you to touch me or – speak to me. Ever!" cried Davina.

Then, all sense fled her and she fell sobbing against his breast.

He waited patiently, staring out over the lake.

After a while her sobs subsided. She raised her head and stared around, as if uncertain as to her whereabouts.

"Are you ready to go inside?" asked Charles calmly.

She passed a hand over her brow. "Y-yes. But not – with you. I am – steady now."

"As you wish, madam." He gave a slight bow and then stiffened.

Something on her bosom had caught his eye. She made to draw her cloak about her but he quickly caught her wrist to prevent her.

"What is that?" he asked, before she could protest.

"T-that?" Looking down, she saw a silver brooch, fashioned in the shape of a pineapple pinned to her bodice.

"I – do not rightly know – it is not mine."

"I have no doubt that it is not yours. May I ask who gave it to you?"

Davina faltered under his cold and enquiring stare.

"J-Jed Barker," she whispered.

Charles's jaw clenched and hardened. "Jed," he murmured abstractedly. "Of course."

"I did not ask for it and do not want it," muttered Davina.

"Then may I take it from you, madam?"

"Take it if you will!" cried Davina. "Take it from me!"

Charles reached forward. His eyes met hers for one stinging moment, one moment in which his fingers hovered at her bosom, one moment in which she cursed the blood that rushed to her face. Then the brooch lay glittering in his palm and it was as if she did not exist.

'What does it matter, I hate him!' she half wept to herself as she stumbled towards the French windows. 'What does it matter?'

Yet as she pushed open the window, she could not help but turn for one last look at his tall figure, outlined now against the rising moon. Of all that had happened to her today, the worst was this. Knowing the perfidy of the man and knowing his habits, her flesh had still burned with pleasure to have his hands so near.

How could she excuse or forgive her own heart, her own too treacherous heart?

CHAPTER EIGHT

All along the driveway, torches burned. Servants had spent a great part of the afternoon driving in the staves. Now the flames flickered in the night breeze like so many glow worms dancing in the dark.

Throughout the ground floor of the house, candles flared in their sconces. Only in the upper storeys were oil lamps lit for the evening.

Downstairs the rooms were fragrant of roses and cedar from great bowls of pot pourri and from huge logs burning in the many hearths.

Supper was in progress. Lord Shelford sat at one end of the table, Davina at the other. In the candlelight, her cheeks bore the gleam of marble, her hair the sheen of silk. Her eyes seemed huge, the irises of a deep and almost mysterious hue. Many a gaze was drawn to her.

Only two men failed to look her way.

Her fiancé, Howard, kept his head low, his eyes on his plate or, with greater frequency, on his glass. All evening, he had avoided being alone with Davina. It was clear he wanted to avoid the topic of the brawl that she had witnessed yesterday. His eye looked somewhat swollen and he seemed generally ill at ease. He spoke so brusquely to his neighbours that in the end they turned away from him to discourse with others.

Charles, meanwhile, sat staring straight ahead, his jaw tight, his gaze hooded. When addressed, he responded with considerable but remote courtesy. Every so often his hand wandered to his breast as if he kept something concealed there, something that troubled him.

Regine, who had devoted so much energy to this event, was sensitive to the strange currents that seemed to pervade the table. Whatever was the matter with Davina and Howard? One would think they had nothing to do with each other! As for Charles, he was as cold as a mummy! At least her Duke was in good form, having found that the Reverend Gee, seated to his left, was extremely interested in the intricacies of cattle breeding.

After supper, there was to be music and dancing in the hall. As the guests prepared to rise, however, Lord Shelford exchanged a glance with Charles and then requested that all the gentlemen present withdraw to the library for a few moments.

The women rustled ahead, whispering to each other behind their fans.

"I have heard that some information has come to light that may at last lead us to the main perpetrator of these attacks," Davina heard Aunt Sarah say as she and Lady Criston passed.

Davina sank onto a chair in the hall. She barely heard the strains of the music around her.

She wondered if the brooch she had yielded to Lord Delverton had anything to do with this recent development. But she quickly dismissed such an idea from her mind. She was certain that he had not mentioned their encounter on the terrace to anyone.

If he had done, her father or Regine would have asked for explanations as to where she had been and why she had returned in such a distressed state.

As it was, the household had been too busy to remark on her absence.

Yet all through supper she could not help but notice the way Lord Delverton's hand constantly strayed to his breast, where she was certain the brooch was hidden. She remembered his response when she explained who had given it to her: "*Jed Barker. Of course.*" Her cheeks reddened every time she thought of what those words meant.

Lord Delverton suspected her of an intrigue with Jed Barker!

Her apparent desire to be rid of the brooch, he may well have read as evidence of a lovers' quarrel. She looked up as the doors to the hall opened and the men returned.

Their faces were grim and determined. She wondered what had been discussed in the library. Her curiosity was soon dispelled by Regine, who, after a brief interchange with their father, hurried over.

"A brooch belonging to Sir Vincent's wife, that was stolen when they were attacked, has been recovered," said Regine excitedly.

"H-how was it recovered?" asked Davina tremulously.

"Oh – Lord Delverton recovered it, though he did not specify how."

Davina closed her eyes in relief – a surprised relief, since she could not see why Lord Delverton should protect his source in this way. She had, after all, treated him with undisguised revulsion!

"Anyway," continued Regine, "Lord Delverton is now convinced he knows the identity of the man behind all the attacks. A posse of men is being sent out to apprehend him."

"W-which men?" enquired Davina.

Regine laughed. "Oh, none of our guests, you may be sure. Papa insisted on that. He would not have us robbed of

121

dancing partners! No, some of the stable hands have gone out. They'll think it great sport! Now – you cannot sit there like a wallflower. Where is Howard? I thought I saw him a moment ago. Ah! Lord Delverton. You'll do. You must partner your sister-to-be, since your brother seems to have disappeared."

Charles hesitated for a second. He bowed and held out his hand, his face set like stone.

"Madam," he said.

Under Regine's pert eye, Davina dared not refuse.

They glided in silence across the floor.

Charles kept his face averted, while Davina stared at her hand resting lightly on his broad, proud shoulders. She had not expected to find herself in this situation. She had determined to avoid this man whom she now considered unprincipled and devious and yet – and yet her heart continued to belie her.

For within moments of being in his arms, she felt as if she was dancing on air. Her blood surged to her fingers where they met his. Where his other hand rested on her waist, her flesh began to burn beneath her bodice. She wished to be gone and yet she wished the music never to end.

As another couple brushed by, Davina's step faltered. In steadying her, Charles could not but meet her gaze.

The look that passed between them was as charged as a night of storm.

His grip on her waist tightened as his eyes seared into hers. She flinched and his hold tightened yet further. His eyes were full of a fire he could not quench. His fingers pressed harder into her bodice. Her own fingers curled and uncurled upon his shoulder as waves of pain alternating with pleasure swept through her. She felt exhausted and exhilarated by such unfamiliar emotions.

The two of them almost came to a standstill there on

the floor, their breath mingling, their lips threatening to meet. Only the sudden, flourishing conclusion of the music and the laughter and applause that followed forced them to stagger apart.

Davina stood, bosom heaving, cheeks flushed, eyes unnaturally bright.

Charles passed a hand across his brow and then stepped back, giving a muted bow.

"Madam. – I must escort you to your seat – "

"Of – course," Davina performed a quick curtsy and turned away. She did not extend her hand for him to take, but she was all too aware that he was at her side. When they reached the row of chairs against the wall, Charles again bowed and, without another word, departed.

Davina, trembling, lifted her fan to her face. When Aunt Sarah sat down beside her and began to question her about the forthcoming wedding, she found she could barely reply. She longed to be alone with her racing thoughts. Then suddenly she turned huge, despairing eyes to her companion.

"Lady Sarah – "

Her companion gave her a quick tap on the knee with her fan. "Oh, come now, you must get used to calling me aunt!"

"Yes, of course. A-aunt Sarah, Have you ever seen gypsy women dance?"

"Gypsy women? I can't say that I – wait, yes, once. I was a girl and I was taken to see some jugglers. There was a gypsy girl there, dancing. Whirling and twirling like a spinning top. A most abandoned manner. The men like that, of course."

The men like that, of course.

Davina sank back in her chair, her heart heavy as lead

again.

Charles meanwhile walked into the hallway and stopped for a moment in the flickering shadows thrown by the candelabra. His features were drawn. How had he allowed himself to be waylaid by Regine and engaged as partner to Davina? *To dance with her!* Nothing could have been further from his mind.

He had asked himself a thousand times why Jed should have given that silver brooch to Davina and only one answer presented itself. It was surely a lover's token! Yet he had not voiced his suspicions.

When, in the library, he had shown the brooch to Lord Shelford and the other men, he had simply said that it had been in Jed Barker's possession – as it surely had. He neglected to mention that he had actually secured it from Davina.

He groaned as he remembered how it had felt to hold her in his arms.

Her body moving with his, the scent of her perfume, the soft touch of her hand, the faint flush in her cheeks when their gaze met – these sensations had almost unmanned him. Almost made him forget that not only was she not his, she was very likely not Howard's, either!

Where the deuce *was* his brother, anyway? He should be mingling with the guests, dancing with his fiancée and aunt and future sister-in-law.

Howard had been understandably dismayed to learn that Jed was implicated in the robberies, but that was no excuse for simply vanishing. He should be at his fiancée's side this evening.

Charles searched from room to room but his brother was not to be found. At last he stepped out on to the terrace and scanned the lawns.

There were no clouds and he could see as far as the

lakeside.

Narrowing his eyes, he started. Surely that was a figure on horseback?

Horse and rider stood facing the house, and he could see in the moonlight that the horse was of a pale hue. As if sensing his gaze, the horse was suddenly wheeled about. It set off at a canter along the lake.

Following its progress, Charles realised that it was not in order to avoid his scrutiny that the rider had turned, but in order to intercept a second figure on horseback, approaching from the direction of the stables. He strained his eyes but could make out no detail of the other figure save that the horse was dark and the rider in an even darker cape.

Could it possibly be Howard? He certainly rode a black horse and he was certainly nowhere in the house. If it was he, what on earth was he doing abandoning the party and his fiancée in this manner?

Musing on what he should do – ride in pursuit or make excuses for Howard's absence – Charles was about to re-enter the house when he was accosted by Lord Shelford on his way out.

"Ah! Delverton! Just the man. I wonder if you would care to take a stroll with me? There is something troubling me – it concerns us both – I should be glad to unburden myself."

The tone in which these words were spoken was so urgent that, with a last glance toward the retreating riders, Charles readily assented.

"Certainly, Lord Shelford."

Seemingly reassured, Lord Shelford relaxed a little. "I must say I am glad to get away from all this merriment. We could walk to the lake. I have a flask of brandy on me. And a couple of first class cigars."

Charles again assented and the two men set off,

walking at first in silence. Ahead of them, in Priory Lake, the reflected moon turned slowly, a pale and lonely orb, seeming to sink and drown in the dark, unruffled waters.

*

As the hands of the clock crept on and there was still no sign of Howard, more and more curious looks were cast Davina's way. She sat in her chair, eyes down, opening and shutting her fan where it lay in her lap. She had no wish to dance again and had refused all offers.

She was aware of the growing concern about her and her cheeks flushed with embarrassment. At the same time she was glad, yes, glad that Howard had not come as expected to lead her out on to the floor. She was afraid to be in his arms and not feel what she had felt in Charles's arms, afraid that Howard would sense her regret.

Regine collapsed on a neighbouring chair, her cheeks red as embers from her exertions. She waved her fan vigorously before her face a moment before addressing her sister.

"I wish you would bestir yourself and dance. It makes me feel guilty to be enjoying it all with you sitting here like a blancmange."

Davina smiled faintly. "A blancmange?"

"Well. All pale and quivering. You are, you know. I can't think where Howard has gone to. It's quite wrong of him to disappear like this. Unless, of course, it's this wretched business that the men are about."

"I thought – the stable hands had been sent out?"

"They have, but you know how our own menfolk are. They'd hunt a fellow as quick as a pheasant. Father and Lord Delverton have disappeared too. I am sure they've sneaked away to join in."

"Y-you are?"

"I am."

"And do we know – exactly who it is – they are hunting?"

Regine leaned closer and spoke behind her fan. "I shouldn't really say as it's not common knowledge but I believe it to be that lout Jed Barker. The stable hands set off in the direction of Lark House and they were hardly going to arrest the cook there, were they?"

Davina was silent for a moment and then rose. "I think I should like to retire."

"Dear girl, you can't be serious. You are the hostess."

"No, Regine, I am hardly that. You have been doing the honours and I shall not be missed. I-I'm very tired. Let me just slip away."

Regine opened her mouth to protest again but Davina was already on her way to the door. Regine snapped shut her fan. Really! The goings-on here this evening. She could not puzzle it all out but one thing was certain. She had never met two people less inclined to seek out each other's company than Howard Delverton and her sister!

Davina made her way quickly to her room. Jess sprang up from her seat before the fire when her mistress entered.

"It's not over already, is it, miss?"

"No, Jess, but I'm tired. Will you unbutton me, please?"

Astonished, Jess did as she was requested. She helped Davina into her nightgown and brushed out her hair before the mirror.

Davina stared at her reflection. What was it that Esmé had called her?

Pale and spoilt.

She thought of Esmé's vivid features, her red-berry

lips, her flashing black eyes, her hair like a raven's plumage, and tears welled in her eyes. Her own face was indeed as white as china and her hair the insipid colour of buttercups!

At last her toilette was completed. Jess turned back the sheets on the bed and Davina climbed in. Jess bobbed a curtsy.

"Anything else, miss?"

"No, thank you, Jess. Good night."

"Goodnight, miss."

The door closed behind Jess. Far, far away the strains of the music floated in the night, barely perceptible below the crackle of the fire in the grate. Jess had quenched all the lamps bar one, which threw out a faltering light.

Davina closed her eyes. She was alone and yet not alone, for the image of Lord Delverton burned beneath her lids. The sheets were cool to the touch and yet her flesh was on fire. Her heart too was like a flaming brand in her breast. She had never felt this way about Felix Boyer nor any of the other young gentlemen who had wooed her in London.

She had never felt this way about Howard. Only Lord Delverton made her blood surge like hot liquid in her veins. What could she do, what *should* she do? To respond so to such a man when she was betrothed to a better!

The shame seemed more than she could bear.

Tears wet her pillow as she tossed and turned. Then the logs shifted in the grate, one or two falling to ashes. Whether it was this that made her open her eyes or something else she was not sure, but she opened her eyes to an unexpected darkness. The lamp that stood on the table by the door had gone out.

It did not trouble her to sleep without a light. She usually did. She had only requested that Jess leave the lamp burning tonight because she expected Regine to look in on her later, full of gossip and intrigue.

Davina rose from her bed. If the wick was spent, it would be better to move the lamp into the other room, rather than have its oily odour hang in the air.

Feeling over the surface of the table, her brow creased. The lamp had gone!

She thought for a moment and then returned to her bed. Jess must have crept in and decided it was safer to take it away. Perhaps she would bring a new one before long.

Davina lay back. She thought she would stay awake all night, but before long she began to drift into sleep.

She therefore did not notice the slow and careful opening of the door to her chamber, nor notice the lamp she thought was extinguished flickering in the room beyond. She did not notice the man who approached her bed nor the satisfaction that crossed his features when he saw that she slept.

She slumbered as he returned to the adjoining room, slumbered as he tilted the lamp until the oil streamed out across the carpet. She slumbered as the burning wick was lowered to meet the dark and viscous liquid.

A whoosh of flame rose in an instant, sending out tongues of fire to lap at curtains, carpets and sofas. Soon a thick, enveloping smoke, having filled Davina's sitting room, began to seep insidiously beneath her bedroom door.

Its black and oily tentacles seemed to feel their way through the air, seeking a victim, any victim, to wrap in their deadly, choking embrace.

*

"Brrrr!" shivered Lord Shelford, as he took out his flask and offered it to Charles who shook his head. Lord Shelford took a draft and smacked his lips.

"Nothing better on a chill evening," he said as he brought out two cigars and handed one to Charles who this time did accept. The two men stood smoking in silence, listening to the lap of water at their feet.

Charles was musing on their conversation as they had walked to the lake.

Lord Shelford had taken a while to voice his concerns. It was as if he was sounding him out, whilst not wishing to offend him with direct questions. How long was it that Charles had been away in Africa? Ten years!

A long time for Howard to be without the guidance of an elder brother.

A handsome young fellow like that, must have had a lot of temptations come his way. And who to turn to, once his father was ill? How long had the father been ill? Some time. So Howard was running the entire estate all that time then, was he not? Who *did* he turn he?

Jed Barker, as he had heard. So how close was the bond with Barker?

And did anyone have any idea of just who Jed was?

Charles answered patiently, with only a suspicion of where all this questioning was leading.

Lord Shelford's last question was the most difficult to address. He explained that Jed had been found wandering in the grounds of Lark House.

"He was old enough to be walking, then?" queried Lord Shelford.

"That's right. Walking but not talking. So there was no sense to be got out of him."

"And who found him, exactly?"

"My father. He was returning from a tour of the estate."

"Walking! Not a – not an illegitimate child, then, abandoned at birth!"

"Indeed not, Lord Shelford," replied Charles. "More

like a child abandoned by parents who could no longer afford to keep him."

"And your father put him into the care of a farmer's widow?"

"Old Mrs. Barker. Yes. She cared for him as best she might. He became a playmate of ours – of Howard's particularly."

Lord Shelford sighed. "Jed being implicated in this rotten business of the robberies must go hard with Howard? Unless – " he hesitated.

Charles looked up sharply and finished for him.

"Unless my brother is also implicated?"

Lord Shelford nodded, a little shame-faced. "I had not wished to come to that and yet – I must."

"I do not for one moment believe that my brother has had any involvement in the robberies."

Lord Shelford sighed. "Why did he make off like that this evening, then? He just disappeared after our meeting in the library. I dare say you do know your brother, but are you sure he hasn't gone to warn Jed that we are on to him?"

Charles considered and answered truthfully. "I am not sure, Lord Shelford." He was thinking of the two riders he had seen earlier, heading for the woods. He was certain one of them was Howard.

"But I will say this," he continued, "although Howard might choose to warn Jed, it would most certainly be out of friendship rather than partnership."

"Humph!" Lord Shelford grunted. "Well, that may be, but it is conspiracy to prevent the course of justice, if that is what he's about. And it's churlish behaviour to my daughter, to desert her in that manner."

"That I grant," responded Charles softly.

"Indeed," proceeded Lord Shelford after a moment,

"his general conduct towards Davina leaves a great deal to be desired. For some days now, I have remarked on his neglect. It is neither malicious nor deliberate but seems rather to be the result of a – lack of firm attachment.

"It is as if his mind – his heart – are elsewhere. And I must admit that Davina herself seems, of late, to have become similarly distracted. This evening at supper I was most disturbed by their mutual disregard. They exchanged not a glance, not a word, all evening. I ask you, sir, is that normal between two young persons?

"Is it normal for a young man to be so unmoved by the young lady he is to marry? Especially when the lady is – and here I beg your pardon, but I think, though her father, I am well able to view her charms with objectivity – especially when, I say, that the lady is such a treasure!"

Charles drew his cloak about him before he replied carefully.

"My brother's attitude does not seem at all reasonable in such circumstances."

"To tell you the truth, Delverton, I was puzzled by his proposal and just as puzzled by her acceptance. With all due respect to your good self, Howard would not have been my choice for my daughter. I doubted he was such as could make her happy and it increasingly seems that I was correct. Why she wants him, I cannot tell."

Charles stared ahead.

"Perhaps she loves him, Lord Shelford."

"Perhaps," he sighed. "She is a girl who can be led by her emotions, I fear." He sighed again. "I always felt she needed a husband of strong character to guide her. Not someone as – as easy going as Howard. The question is, Delverton, should we take it upon ourselves to intervene?"

Charles hesitated.

"Lord Shelford," he said quietly after a moment, "I

suspect that fate may well intervene for us."

He looked surprised. "You do?"

"Yes. We should let events run their course, at any rate."

This last exchange had brought the two men to the lake's edge. Now they stood, cigars glowing, looking out over the water. The moon lay ghostly and silent beneath its surface. Lord Shelford flicked away his ash and then gestured towards the woods beyond.

"Do you know about the tomb in there?" he asked.

"I do."

"Queer story. Davina was much taken with it." Lord Shelford drew deeply on his cigar and its point glimmered brightly in the darkness. "Wasn't there some rumour that Evelyn Felk had a child?"

Charles turned. "There was."

"Well – couldn't Jed Barker be that child?"

"You forget," he replied, "that Evelyn Felk drowned herself some three years before Jed was found wandering on our estate. If Jed were her child, where was he for those intervening years?'

Lord Shelford shrugged. "I don't know. But it's a mystery and the baby was never found, after all."

"It was believed," said Charles softly, "that she took the child with her when she drowned herself. It was so small it was never discovered in the lake. Another story was that she killed it and buried the body in an unmarked grave."

Lord Shelford whistled sadly. "I have never heard that theory. In which case, we will have to discover other parentage for our rogue, Jed." He threw his cigar into the lake, where it hissed like a water snake. "Would you care to stroll on?"

When Charles did not reply, he turned and was

surprised to see that his companion seemed rooted to the spot, his eyes fixed intently on the farther shore.

Lord Shelford followed his gaze and started. A figure stood there – a figure in a cloak. Even from where they stood, they could see that the figure was that of a woman who had dopped the hood of the cloak to reveal a shock of white hair.

Charles recognised her as the old woman who had been at the fireside at Esmé's cottage. It seemed that she recognised him as well, for she was gesticulating wildly.

"Is that female – calling to us?" asked Lord Shelford. "I can hear shouting."

"It cannot be she that you hear. She is over a quarter of a mile away."

"Nevertheless, I hear something – very faintly," persisted Lord Shelford.

"Indeed I hear more than one – "

Both men turned, for now Charles heard it too, voices crying out wildly from the direction of the house.

Alhough Davina's room was at the front of the house and they were facing the back, they could see in an instant the cause of the consternation.

Above the roof rose a plume of smoke and the air was glowing red.

The east wing of Priory Park was on fire!

CHAPTER NINE

Charles, being younger and more fleet of foot, reached the scene of the conflagration first.

Housemaids were running hither and thither, in helpless panic. Jess sat rocking to and fro on a fallen log, her green shawl over her head. Nearby Mrs. Crouch was lying in a state of shock against an old oak.

Parfitt, meanwhile, his collar undone and his sleeves rolled up, was attempting valiantly to organise a team of fire-fighters, but he lacked troops.

The strongest hands – those belonging to men who worked in the stables or in the fields – had been sent off earlier in pursuit of Jed Barker.

Parfitt greeted Charles with relief. "Thank God you are here, my Lord!" he cried. "We are severely under-manned."

He looked round wildly. "Where are the ladies?" he asked in a tight voice.

Parfitt ran a sleeve over his brow. "That's just the thing, my Lord. Miss Regine and Lady Sarah – they are accounted for – but Miss Davina – "

Charles staggered where he stood. "She is – in the house?"

Parfitt gestured towards Davina's bedroom window.

"We can't get to her, my Lord. And we can't seem to rouse her."

Pale as death, Charles looked at the house. The room adjoining Davina's bedroom was fiercely aglow. There could be no doubt that now, even now, smoke must be pouring over Davina's sleeping figure.

Lord Shelford hobbled into view, his face ashen. One look confirmed his worst fears.

"My – my daughters?" he croaked. "Davina? Regine?"

"Papa, Papa, I am here!" Regine rushed out from a nearby summer house where she had been sheltering and flung herself sobbing into her father's arms. "I am safe, Papa. But Davina – poor Davina – she is trapped!"

Lord Shelford groaned in despair. "Trapped? Then I must try to reach her."

Regine clung to his arm. "You can't, Papa!" she wailed. "The Duke – my dear Duke – tried to get to her along the corridor, but he was overcome by smoke."

"The Duke was indeed driven back," confirmed Parfitt. "Then we brought a ladder, but the ground floor rooms have such high ceilings the ladder wasn't long enough to reach the first storey windows."

"By God," roared Lord Shelford, "do you expect me to stand here and watch my daughter die!"

"You will not have to endure that," came Charles's strained but resolute voice.

He had been scanning the house and was now removing his jacket.

"Do you see that parapet running under the first floor windows? If I can get Davina there, she will at least be out of the way of the flames. I can secure a rope to that low chimney on the left and – try to bring her down that way."

Lord Shelford clutched his brow, staring upwards at the glowing windows. "But how will you get up there when the ladder is too short?"

"That tree over there." He threw his jacket to the ground and began to roll up his sleeves. "There are two or three branches that extend towards the house."

"Surely they are too thin to walk along – " began Parfitt but a look from Charles silenced him.

The Duke of Bedley was now making his way across the grass, leaning heavily on the arm of Aunt Sarah. "What is happening here?" he called out.

"Lord Delverton – is attempting to reach Davina!" cried Regine.

"If only I were younger I'd try it myself!" moaned Lord Shelford, tears welling in his eyes.

Jess, who had long since taken the shawl from her head to stare dazedly at the proceedings, began to cry loudly.

"Oh, do save Miss Davina, do!"

"I need no urging," Charles murmured, moving off quickly towards the tree. Parfitt, shaking his head mournfully, hurried away to find a rope.

Charles leapt for the lower part of the tree. He managed to grasp a branch and haul himself up, painfully aware that the wrist injured when he was attacked was not as strong as it might be. Below, anxious, upturned faces watched his progress. He climbed swiftly to the middle of the tree, where some of the branches most nearly met the walls of the house.

On closer view, these branches were even more slender than he had supposed. He tested each with his foot, realising with growing despair that it was unlikely that any of them would bear his weight. Yet he needed to walk out along one of them if he was to reach the parapet.

With steely nerve he began to edge out along what he hoped was the toughest branch. He could feel it bend beneath him. He hesitated, wondering if he should drop to all fours, and then heard an ominous cracking sound.

As the branch split under his feet he hurled himself backwards, towards the trunk.

His body caught amid the boughs and he began to slither. He thrust out a hand to grasp for support but missed. It was only on the lowest bough that he managed to break his fall and drop to the ground with no great injury.

He was on his feet in an instant and ready to begin the ascent again, but a familiar voice restrained him.

"Stop! You must let *me* go."

He turned, his breast heaving, a lock of hair lank over his brow. His gaze widened as Esmé stepped forward, gold bracelets tinkling about her ankles.

"You!" he exclaimed.

"Yes, I," replied Esmé.

The onlookers regarded each other each other in confusion. Who was this gypsy woman whom Lord Delverton seemed to know? Only Regine gave a start of possible recognition, for she remembered Davina's anxiety about just such a creature as this who now stood before them.

Charles passed a bewildered hand across his brow.

"I do not know what you are doing here, but – I cannot allow you for one moment to endanger yourself in the manner you are suggesting."

"There is little time to lose," said Esmé softly. "Let Esmé go in your place."

"Madam!" cried Charles. "There is not a gentleman on earth who would allow such a thing."

"But there is," came another familiar voice, and Howard stepped into view. White as a sheet, his features

138

drawn, he nevertheless spoke with resolution.

"I would let her do it *because she can*. She is as light as a feather on her feet and she has trained – on the tightrope."

His voice fell away as he and Charles stared at each other. The question of how Howard knew anything at all about Esmé passed through Charles's mind but he put it quickly aside.

"I cannot permit it," he said firmly, turning to the tree.

"For God's sake, brother, let her do what she can to save Davina," muttered Howard. "It is only your pride that is preventing her."

Lord Shelford wrung his hands. "You cannot make it out along the branch, Delverton. Let this woman try."

"Trust me," asserted Esmé.

Charles looked into her eyes for a moment and then nodded reluctantly.

"Very well," he said gruffly. "Here comes Parfitt with a rope. He's made one end into a noose. Is that knot tight, Parfitt? Good.

"Now Esmé, you can see that low chimney to the left – it's the smoking room chimney. Once you get Davina out onto the parapet – attach the noose end of the rope to that chimney and I will climb up and bring Davina down. Can you carry the rope now or shall I throw it up to you?"

"I will take it with me," breathed Esmé. "Loop it about my neck."

Charles did so, his eyes never leaving hers.

"God go with you," he murmured.

Esmé gave a brief, reassuring smile and ran to the tree. She climbed swiftly and within seconds was opposite the first storey parapet of the house. She scrutinised each bough carefully before making her choice.

Arms outstretched on either side to maintain her balance, she stepped forward as lightly as a gazelle. She slid first one foot forward, then the other, testing each move as if she was on a tightrope. The bough dipped beneath her as she went, but held.

"She's made it!" Lord Shelford gasped as Esmé paused, measured the distance, and leapt from bough to parapet in one fleet move.

All eyes were fixed on Esmé, as she edged along the parapet towards Davina's window. All hands were clasped in the same prayer.

Let rescue not be too late!

*

Davina lay as still as if in a tomb.

Smoke eddied about her, drifting like wraiths in the breeze from the half open window. She sensed nothing. Already the oily fumes mingled with her breath and were seeping into her lungs with deadly intent.

The hand that reached for her shoulder had to shake her hard. Yet Davina barely stirred. The voice that urged her to rise did not penetrate her deep, unhealthy sleep. Only when she was dragged from her bed towards the window did she begin to respond, her breast heaving as she gasped for air.

"Wake up! You must wake!" Esmé shook Davina as if she was a rag doll. "I cannot carry you out. You must wake up!"

Davina's eyes fluttered but did not open. Glancing round, Esmé picked up a pitcher of water that stood nearby and dashed its contents into Davina's face. Davina gasped, spluttered and looked about her in bewilderment.

"Come with me" ordered Esmé.

Seeing who commanded her, Davina drew back. "No

– no," she muttered.

Esmé crushed Davina against her, her lips to Davina's ear.

"Obey Esmé or die," she hissed.

Davina's gaze widened. "D-die?"

"Do you not see the smoke? Do you not hear the flames? There is not a moment to lose."

Davina turned to look at the room behind her. The smoke had gathered in a louring cloud, filling the room. She staggered back against Esmé, who spun her round and thrust her at the window.

"Out," called Esmé, "out."

Davina clambered unsteadily out onto the parapet, teetering back with terror as she beheld the drop. Esmé scrambled up beside her, the rope that had been around her neck now in her hands.

"We must go this way, to the right," she urged. "Lord Delverton pointed out a chimney – "

"L-Lord Delverton?" Bewildered and apprehensive as she was, Davina nevertheless caught at the name wildly. "He – is down there?"

"Yes. Your fiancé too and your father."

Davina pressed her back to the wall and closed her eyes. She was utterly humiliated at the idea that Lord Delverton had sent Esmé, his lover, to her rescue.

"Follow me," came Esmé's voice.

Davina opened her eyes. Esmé was edging away along the parapet, her back to the wall, feeling her way with her feet. Davina swallowed. Her legs trembled but she knew that all eyes below were on her. She was determined not to seem to lack courage, especially when her rival was so fearless.

Palms flat against the stone behind her, she began to

inch her way after Esmé.

Esmé reached the low roof of the smoking room. Near the apex, the brick chimney rose some five foot into the air. Leaning out from the wall, Esmé flung up the rope. The first throw fell short. She tried again and this time the rope slithered down over the chimney and caught.

There were cheers from below. Esmé now let go of the loose end of the rope. It slid down the roof and over the edge, to dangle a foot or so from the ground. Charles rushed forward and tested his weight on it.

"It's holding well," he shouted.

Esmé turned to Davina, who had reached the edge of the parapet and stood gazing out over the smoking room roof.

"He will climb up and carry you down," she said. "I will follow."

Davina stiffened. "No!" she said firmly. "No. I will climb down by myself."

Esmé raised an eyebrow. "I don't think he will agree."

"I do not care if he agrees or not," retorted Davina. "Besides, the rope may be strong enough for one, but how do we know if it is strong enough for two?"

Esmé shrugged. "You may be right. But can you do it?"

"I used to climb ropes as a little girl," replied Davina. She called to the anxious group below. "I am going to climb down myself."

"No," cried Lord Shelford. "I forbid you!"

In answer, Davina caught at the rope where it hung from the chimney and, gripping it in her hands, used it to lower herself down the smoking room roof. She reached the guttering and rested for a moment, flat against the tiles.

Then she pushed off again.

She had indeed climbed ropes as a girl – ropes that hung from low branches, with her mother ready to catch her. This was different. She swung in the air, shocked at the sudden drag on her arms.

She had a vision of a sack of flour she had once seen lowered out of a mill window. Bump, bump, bump all the way to the bottom. She flushed as she thought of Lord Delverton watching her. Did she look like a sack of flour? She was sure she weighed more. Her arms ached already and she had not even begun the descent.

Esmé's voice called softly to her. "Put one hand above the other. Wrap your ankles about the rope. That will help."

Shame engulfed Davina, but she followed Esmé's instructions and immediately felt she had more control of the rope. Hand over hand, she made her way down. It seemed to take an eternity. Blood pounded in her ears so that she barely heard the words of encouragement from below.

More than once she was tempted to let herself fall. Perhaps she would merely float to the ground, like gossamer! Anything, anything rather than this strain! Her arms would surely be pulled out of their sockets!

Exhausted, she paused, releasing one hand to wipe her brow. The other hand, red and stinging from the coarse rope, was not strong enough to hold her. With a cry, she fell, with no idea of how much space was left between herself and the ground.

Strong arms caught her. Strong arms crushed her to a powerful breast.

"Thank God. Thank God, my darling. You are safe," a voice murmured against her hair.

Before she had even opened her eyes to see who it was, she felt herself wrested away. Now her father's beard tickled her face as he covered her with kisses. Regine meanwhile plucked at her sleeve, squealing with undisguised

143

delight.

"I'm so happy, dear sister, I'm so happy."

Davina wriggled free of her father's ardent embrace. Her mind was in a turmoil.

"Papa, the fire – how did it start?"

Lord Shelford frowned uneasily. "It seems – the east wing corridor was – drenched with oil from one of the lamps."

Davina paled. "By accident?"

Lord Shelford and the Duke exchanged a glance. "We – do not know, my dear."

"But someone must have then set a match to it!" cried Davina. "*That* could not have been an accident."

"Hush now, hush," urged her father. "What does it matter! You are safe, thanks to that – that gypsy woman."

Davina raised her eyes to the smoking room roof, where Esmé had began her descent. She almost drifted down the rope, Davina noted ruefully.

Lowering her gaze, Davina caught sight of Lord Delverton. There he stood, watching Esmé avidly. Beside him – Howard – his eyes feverish as he too watched the descent of the beautiful gypsy.

Esmé reached the ground and the two brothers rushed to her.

Davina bit her lip.

Had she been wrong? Was her fiancé as enamoured of Esmé as Lord Delverton?

She might have dwelt longer on this thought, but an agitated cry arose around her.

"Look there – on the roof – look there!"

Everyone turned. Above the rooms where the fire raged, brandishing one of the torches that had earlier marked out the route to Priory Park, stood a wild and dishevelled figure. Shirt torn and scorched, teeth and eyes gleaming in a face blackened with soot, it was a few moments before anyone recognised him. Then, with one accord, an astonished cry ran through the watching crowd.

"It's Jed up there. It's Jed Barker."

"Good God, man, come down!" shouted Lord Shelford. "You'll be killed!"

Jed ran along the apex of the roof, as lithe as a cat, until he was directly above the crowd. He leered down at their incredulous faces.

"How do you like my handiwork, eh?" he screeched. "It don't do to underestimate Jed, you know."

"What have you done, man?" cried Lord Shelford with a horrified groan. "And why? Why destroy my house?"

"Why? *Why*? Because it's not your house, Shelford. It's mine. Mine by right, mine by blood."

"How can it be yours?" cried the bewildered Lord Shelford. "I bought it fair and square from the Felk estate."

"But they had no right to sell it!" screamed Jed. "Not while Jed Barker breathed! They had no right. It were mine. And if I couldn't have it the right way, I might have had it through your daughter, but that Delverton got in the way. Now no one shall have it and no one shall have your lovely daughter either!"

"That is one triumph you shall not have, Jed Barker," trumpeted Lord Shelford in utter relief. "Can't you see she is safe here at my side?"

Jed squinted. When he recognised Davina, pale but composed, staring up at him, he howled like an injured dog.

"Barker, come down!" commanded Charles. "Don't be a fool."

In answer Jed flung the burning torch into the air. The

145

crowd scattered as it dropped flaming into their midst.

"Boy, pretty boy, come down." A quavering voice, barely audible, rose into the air. Davina heard it and turned.

An old woman in a cloak, hair white as ash, stretched a claw-like hand towards the fire.

"Boy, pretty boy, come down," the old woman repeated. She was distracted for a moment only as Esmé moved to her side and gently put an arm about her shoulders. Then her milky eyes turned once again to the roof.

The crowd gasped as flames shot up through the roof just below Jed, who seeing them, threw back his head and roared.

There was a scream from the old woman as the roof beneath Jed collapsed. With another roar he disappeared into a raging hell of flame.

The air before Davina seemed to blur. Blood rushed from her cheeks. She swayed once on her feet and then fell.

The bright flames, the noise, the mad cries of Jed were gone. In their place was silence and a darkness beyond measure.

*

"You're awake at last, miss," said Jess, peering down at Davina.

Davina, her eyes barely open, stared up at Jess and then above her to the fringes of a scarlet canopy.

"This – this isn't my bed, Jess. Where am I?"

"You're at Lark House, miss," replied Jess, drawing open the curtains.

"After you fainted, Lord Delverton carried you to his carriage and ordered the coachman to bring you here."

"L-Lord Delverton?"

"Yes, miss. Your sister and Lady Sarah are here too.

And that awful Mrs. Crouch. Your father stayed behind with the other men to help put out the fire."

Davina fell back against the pillow as the full memory of last night flooded back to her.

"Jed Barker! Why did he do it, Jess?"

"I can tell you that, miss. The Duke of Bedley came by this morning with all the news. It's quite flown round the house."

Davina struggled upright on her pillow again. "Then please let me hear it, Jess," she pleaded.

With just a hint of self-importance, Jess drew a chair up to the bedside and began to recount events as she had heard them.

"The men had struggled for hours to contain the fire, but if it had not started to rain heavily, Priory Park would have been razed to the ground. As it was, the east wing was entirely destroyed. Meanwhile, the old woman who had appeared out of nowhere was taken aside and questioned. Her words came out all topsy-turvey, but gradually her story was pieced together.

"The wonder was, it seemed Jed *did* have a claim of sorts on Priory Park for, as the old woman soon revealed, *he was the illegitimate son of Evelyn Felk!*"

Davina gasped with astonishment.

"The old woman is Martha, Lady Felk's maid. She it was who delivered Lady Felk's baby, in secret, after her husband and lover were dead.

"The deaths had sorely unhinged Lady Felk's mind. She was convinced that her late husband's family would kill her baby if they discovered him. So she instructed Martha to take the child to live in the woods."

Jess continued, "Martha kept him there for nigh on three years and a lonely three years it was, for once her –

mistress was drowned – and what a shock that was to Martha – nobody knew that she and the child were there.

"Imagine those winters," shuddered Jess, "with the candles guttering and the wind howling down the chimneys like a pack of wolves. And all the time Martha was grieving for her dead mistress, whom she had loved dearly.

"Every week she put fresh flowers on her grave, long after everyone else had forgotten the grave was there. *I reckon Martha's own mind started to go then*," said Jess, "*for by all accounts it's like a sheet flapping in the wind now.*

"Martha poached game and foraged for fruit and nuts, but life in the woods was hard. She felt the boy ought to be brought up at a big house, like the one his mother had lived in, and he should have leather shoes and a cape to wear in the bad weather.

"So one day she abandoned him in the grounds of Lark House. She'd heard that the master there was a kind man. And so it proved, for he found a home for the boy, though it wasn't in the big house at all.

"Martha used to lurk about the Lark House estate to see how the boy progressed, but she never approached him nor allowed herself to be discovered. She too believed that the Felk family would wish to harm him, even though there was only a decrepit old cousin alive, who wouldn't have the strength to lift a tuning fork, let alone any kind of weapon! She believed the boy was safe if only *she* knew he was the son of Lady Felk and if only *she* knew his father was a gypsy!"

"A gypsy!" gulped Davina.

"So it seems," said Jess.

She continued her tale.

"One day, Jed turned up at the cottage in the woods. It so happened that he'd followed Lord Delverton there – curious to discover the identity of the 'woodsman's daughter' – but old Martha didn't know that.

"She thought he had remembered her and come looking for her, so she let him see that she recognised him. She called him 'pretty boy', 'Lady Evie's pretty boy'. It didn't take him long to put two and two together.

"Maybe he wasn't so surprised. Maybe he often used to wonder if there wasn't a connection between the illegitimate child of Lady Felk and the child found wandering the grounds of Lark House. It was only those missing three years and the fact that it was a toddler who was discovered and not a baby, that made a connection seem unlikely.

"He always did act as if he was a cut above the rest of us," concluded Jess with a sniff.

Davina sat back in wonder at all she had heard. It was clear that once Jed discovered who he was, he was determined to do anything to acquire what he believed was his. In his tortured mind he even imagined himself marrying the heiress of Priory Park, herself!

She was lucky to have escaped him that afternoon in the woods. Yet she could not help but pity him. His had been a terrible end, with perhaps only one person amid the crowd of witnesses to truly grieve for him.

"What will happen to Martha?" she mused.

"She's been taken to Lalham Convent to be looked after by the nuns. She didn't want to return to the woods, now that Jed won't be there for her to keep an eye on."

Davina shook her head. "Poor Jed," she sighed.

"Don't you go feeling sorry for him, miss!" snorted Jess. "His rooms were searched last night by the men sent out after him. They found a lot of stolen articles. Jed was the leader of the very brigands who attacked Lord Delverton!"

Davina reeled in astonishment. "But why would he

want to kill Lord Delverton?"

"He was jealous when Lord Delverton returned from Africa to take over the running of the estate. Up to then he was cock of the walk, for he always had great influence over Master Howard. He got a lot of money out of Master Howard. No, Jed Barker was always a bad lot, miss. Must have been his gypsy blood."

Davina looked sternly at her. "You mustn't say that, Jess. Please remember it was a gypsy who saved me last night!"

"Yes, and we're all grateful, but who knows what her motivation was? Me, I wouldn't trust a woman like that. If you ask me, she was hand in glove with Jed. She admitted that he often used to visit her tribe when they camped at Ledger's fields.

"I reckon she was in on the robberies and when she saw the way things were going with Jed last night, she decided she'd better throw in her lot with you and your father. Your father's rich, so she could be pretty sure of a reward for saving you. No one would suspect her. They'll be all over her, the men, just as they were last night. All of them."

"A-all?" repeated Davina, her mind in turmoil.

"All, miss," said Jess firmly. "Especially Lord Delverton. After he handed us into the carriage, he went straight back to her to see how she was. No, I wouldn't trust that Esmé one inch."

'*Esmé, Esmé,*' thought Davina in silent despair. 'All trails seemed in the end to lead to the beautiful, fearless gypsy. *She* hadn't fainted like Davina when Jed fell screaming to his death! Yet Jess was surely right, Esmé was nothing more than a common thief! That ruby ring on her finger was part of the spoils from the robberies. It was given to her by Jed, not Lord Delverton!'

This last idea brought no comfort to Davina. It was

clear from what Jess had just told her that Lord Delverton was deeply involved with the gypsy.

Her beauty turned all men's heads. She would turn her own father's head! He would reward Esmé with money or jewellery, and then she would disappear, laughing at everyone over her shoulder. None of the men would notice the ruby ring on her finger, for they would be too busy staring at her face! That was if Esmé had not removed the ring before ever appearing at Priory Park!

She had to warn her father – Lord Delverton – Howard. She had to warn them that Esmé was not what she seemed.

That this view might diminish their regard for the gypsy was no small part of Davina's decision.

Jess started as Davina began to struggle from her bed.

"Where are you going to, miss? You should rest after all the drama of yesterday. I was about to bring up your breakfast."

"I don't want any breakfast!" said Davina, feeling about the floor with her feet. "I am going home for breakfast. Jess, where are my slippers?"

"At Priory Park, miss," replied Jess. "At least – at least – "

She could not continue. Davina instantly understood. Her slippers were not at Priory Park. They weren't anywhere. They were burned, along with all her clothes and books and hats and shoes and paintings.

And when she thought of paintings, one in particular rose in Davina's mind. The portrait of Evelyn Felk, Jed's mother, destroyed in the very same flames that had devoured her son!

CHAPTER TEN

As Davina rode out through the gates of Lark House, she anxiously scanned the black clouds on the horizon. They hung heavy and inert, but she decided that she could reach Priory Park long before the portended storm broke.

A mile or so along the road a young man hailed her and asked whether Lord Delverton was at home, for he had a letter to deliver to him. Davina hesitated and then replied that he was not at home but at Priory Park. Since that was her own destination, she added, she would be happy to take him the letter. The young man handed it over and Davina continued on her way.

Her heart sank as Priory Park hove into view.

The east wing was a blackened ruin. Charred timber and rubble was all that remained. An acrid smell hung in the air.

She found her father in the library, with Charles. They did not at first notice her, as they were in deep conversation by the fire. She was shocked at the sight of their drawn, ashen features.

"Papa!" she cried.

Her father leapt to his feet and swept her up into a tight embrace.

Behind him, Charles rose slowly from his chair.

"I am glad to see you, my dearest daughter!"

murmured her father. "But you should not have come until you were sent for."

"I know, Papa. But I had to come. Really I did." Her hand strayed to her bonnet and began to twist its strings through her fingers. "Th-there is something I must tell you. But Howard should hear it too. Wh-where is he, Papa?"

Lord Shelford and Charles glanced at each other.

"I am not sure, my dear." He took his daughter's elbow and guided her to a sofa. "I shall order you some tea and then I advise you to return immediately to Lark House."

"Not until I have said what I came to say, Papa!" Davina took a deep breath and then plunged bravely on. "It – it's about Esmé. I believe you are gravely deceived as to her – true character."

"What exactly have you heard, Davina?" he asked gently.

"Heard? Nothing, Papa. It's just that – I have become convinced that she is nothing more than a thief. A thief who was involved with Jed and – his plot to murder Lord Delverton."

Charles's brow darkened. "What is this?" he questioned.

Davina twisted at her bonnet strings. "Did you not see the ring she wears? Such a ring as she could never have procured, but by – nefarious means!"

With an exclamation that denoted utter disdain for this suggestion, Charles turned and walked to the window.

"You don't believe me!" cried Davina, looking from Charles to her father in despair. "Then ask her yourself, Papa, how she came to possess such a valuable jewel. Summon her here and ask her yourself!"

Lord Shelford wiped his brow. "We cannot summon Esmé, my dear. She has disappeared."

Davina rose to her feet in dismay. "Disappeared? Without a reward? No, Papa! She has helped herself to more than she thought you would give her, of that I am certain. Have you counted the – the forks and the spoons and the snuffboxes and – and Regine's pearls and Mrs. Crouch's hatpins? Have you?"

"Hush, Davina, hush," he urged. "You are becoming hysterical."

"Papa, I am not. I just can't believe – refuse to believe – that Esmé left our house with nothing!"

"She did not leave with – *nothing*," replied Lord Shelford miserably.

"Then what *did* she leave with, Papa?"

He cast a desperate look towards Charles who detached himself from the window and walked forward. His tone was grave.

"Madam, Esmé left with neither silver nor gold, pearls nor hatpins. What she did leave with was your fiancé. She left with my dishonourable brother, Howard."

Davina stepped back, her eyes on his. "H-Howard?"

"The cad has bolted!" Lord Shelford broke out, unable to restrain his feelings.

Davina stared. "I-I see. He has gone. With her. I see."

That Charles was, in a sense, as bereft as she, was of no consolation to Davina. She felt nothing but utter humiliation that he should be privy to her abandonment. She began to back towards the door.

"Davina, Davina!" Her father stretched out his hand to her. "Where are you going?"

"I don't know. Home. Oh. I *am* home. Somewhere. I don't know. I DON'T KNOW!"

With that last, despairing crescendo, Davina turned

and fled from the room and the expressionless gaze of Charles, Lord Delverton.

*

Evelyn Felk's tombstone was cold. The lichen that covered it was moist against Davina's cheek as she lay there sobbing.

Nobody loved her, nobody. From being the belle of London society she had become the discarded fiancée. She had never loved Howard, but she *had* supposed that he loved her. Now she had lost everything.

Sobs shook her body. Her fingers clutched at the lichen. Her hair, loosened from her bonnet, spread over the grey stone like a mantle of gold. She wished she was as still and cold as Evelyn Felk!

Black clouds rolled in overhead. The sky churned above the trees. Rain began falling, in shards of ice. Davina made no attempt to shelter.

Soon she was barely conscious, her dress soaked, her body thrashed mercilessly by the hail.

She made no sound as, some time later, a cloak was thrown about her and she was lifted into strong, determined arms.

Her eyelids fluttered open for a moment as she was placed gently onto the back of a horse. She was dimly aware of someone mounting the saddle behind her.

With a moan she fell back against a strong and silent breast. The motion of the horse, urged into a steady walk through the drenched woods, lulled her into a deep, untroubled sleep.

She did not waken until she was lifted from the horse. She heard a door kicked open and glimpsed the edge of a thatched eave as she was carried across a threshold. In a daze she lifted her head. There was a red pitcher on a table,

155

painted candlesticks on a mantel, and a shawl thrown in disarray across a chair!

Esmé's cottage! It must be Howard who had carried her here!

Incensed, Davina began to flail in her abductor's arms, beating her fists on his shoulder.

"Let – me – go. How dare you bring me here, Howard! Let – me – go."

"Madam, be still!" urged a stern voice.

Deposited unceremoniously onto a bed, Davina found herself staring up into the stony features of – Charles! There was a sardonic twist to his lips at her astonishment.

"I am – sorry to disappoint you, madam, but as you see, it is not Howard you have to thank for bringing you here, but I. Your humble servant, Charles Delverton."

Davina struggled upright, her breast heaving.

"W-would Lord Delverton care to inform me *why* he has brought me *here*? He must know that this is the last place on earth I would wish to be. And he should know that he is the last person on earth I would wish as company."

Charles looked strangely tired as he replied. "I had surmised that, madam."

He crossed to where a shift and a worsted cloak hung on a hook and brought the two garments to the bed.

"You must take off those wet clothes," he suggested.

Davina stiffened.

"Since you consider yourself my captive, madam," he said coolly, "you must perforce obey me. I command you to remove your clothes and robe yourself in these."

He dropped the shift and cloak into Davina's lap and turned away. He knelt at the hearth and began to set a fire.

Realising that she was indeed very wet and cold, Davina began to undo her bodice. As she did so, a sealed paper fluttered to the floor.

The letter for Lord Delverton that had been entrusted to her by the boy, on the road to Priory Park! She had forgotten it completely! Whatever her personal feelings towards him, this was a lapse of good manners. She hoped the letter did not contain urgent information.

"L-Lord Delverton."

"Madam?"

"I neglected to give you this. It was handed to me this morning on my way home – "

He took the letter and turned it over in his hand.

"After such a lapse of time!" he exclaimed.

He might have opened the letter there and then had Davina not begun to shiver. He regarded her in alarm.

"Let me find something to dry your hair." Laying aside the letter he picked up the shawl, Esmé's shawl, that hung in disarray over the chair!

"Madam, if I may?"

Davina looked up at him. In the firelight, his expression had softened.

His eyes burned with an unmistakably tender concern. Almost with relief, she bent her head to his touch. She felt herself tremble as he gently began to dry her hair.

Rain still pattered at the window. The logs began to crackle in the hearth. It seemed as if there were just the two of them in the whole, wide world.

"W-will you tell me – why you brought me here?" Davina asked dreamily.

"I did not set out with that intention. I happened to stumble across you in the glade. I chose to continue on here without delay because I believed Howard and Esmé may have come here prior to leaving the area. I wished to – to confront them. But it seems they have already fled."

Davina's heart, burgeoning with hope that he might in some way care for her after all, plummeted once more.

"No doubt you – you desired them to separate," she commented unhappily, certain that Charles wished Esmé to return to him.

"I should have thought, madam," he replied in surprise, "that you would have desired the same."

Davina was about to reply when he suddenly raised his finger to his lips. She shrank apprehensively into the shadows.

There was a rustle outside and the door heaved open.

Howard and Esmé, their clothes dripping, their arms full of bags and parcels, stood on the threshold.

Seeing Charles, Howard scowled and threw down his load. A small portmanteau burst open, spilling its contents. A sword clattered from its scabbard.

Howard stared defiantly at his brother.

"I'm not going back, d'ye hear?" he cried. "I've thrown in my lot with Esmé and that's the end of it."

In one swift move Charles recovered the sword from the floor and was holding its steel tip under Howard's chin.

"By God, that is not the end of it, brother!" he seethed. "You will explain your conduct to me or I'll not answer for the consequences."

"S-steady on there, Charles," muttered Howard nervously. "I don't mind telling you – what's been afoot – but put that sword away, do."

Charles lowered the weapon but did not put it away.

"Come in and defend yourself, then, if you can," he bellowed murderously.

"I – went to collect some things from home first," Howard explained, gesturing at the items scattered over the floor. "Nobody saw me. I crept in – threw everything out of the window to Esmé – and crept out again. Easy as eating meat pie."

Charles regarded him with distaste and motioned him to a chair.

Esmé followed him. Her eyes, keener than Howard's in the dim firelight, espied Davina, motionless in the corner.

"You!" she exclaimed, in evident dismay.

"Yes, Davina," repeated Charles, his voice as hard as iron. He leaned against the edge of the table, his eyes dark and cold as he looked at his brother. "Well, Howard," he growled. "Let us hear your sorry tale."

Howard ran a hand through his hair.

"It's like this," he started. "About a year and a half ago, Jed was doing some business with gypsies over at Ledger's field. I went along with him. And that is when I first saw Esmé."

Davina glared while Charles raised an eyebrow in undisguised surprise.

"You have known her – that long?"

Howard nodded. "She was dancing and singing and I thought her the most beautiful creature in the world. After that night, I often visited the camp. I fell in love with her. And she fell in love with me. I gave her a ring, the one Mama left to me to give to any future – wife. Esmé has it still."

Davina felt momentarily chastened. So Esmé had not stolen the ring after all!

"I – followed her about the country, wherever her family went," resumed Howard. "Then Father took a turn for the worse. It became difficult to get away from Priory Park.

"I had been running the estate for a while, but now I was in complete charge. And I started to see how – how much debt we were in. Jed started on at me. He said I had to give up Esmé – I needed to marry into money. Then Father died and you came home, brother. I was sure you would disapprove of my liaison so I – sent Esmé word that – our relations were severed."

"*You sent word*! Bravo," exclaimed Charles with disdain. "You could not tell her to her face?"

"If he had come to Esmé with those words, she would have killed him!" asserted Esmé imperiously.

Howard flashed her an admiring glance. "You see, Charles? I knew my Esmé too well to risk confronting her! *She'll forget after a while*, I thought, *and no harm done*."

"But he did not know you so well, did he?" Charles said to Esmé.

"No!" replied Esmé fiercely. "Once a gypsy promises herself to a man, only death can break that promise! For weeks Howard did not come. I was so unhappy. Then my father arranged a bridegroom for me.

"So I told him I loved another – an outsider – " Esmé sobbed. "I was banished! Banished! I came to these woods and found this cottage. The old woman was not troubled to have me here so I stayed.

"I knew Howard lived on the other side of the woods. But I did not go to him. I waited for fate to bring him to me! I rescued *you*, Lord Delverton, and discovered you were his brother! Then came – the bad luck man!"

Charles looked at Howard. "The bad luck man?"

"Jed," explained Howard. "He followed you the day you brought the horse to Esmé and when the two of you returned from a ride he was waiting for you. Remember?"

Charles nodded grimly.

"When Jed told us that Howard was to marry, I wanted to die!' cried Esmé. "I sent you away, Lord Delverton, because I did not want you to see how much I wanted to die! After you left, Jed told me all that the old woman had told him.

"Everything was changed, he said. Priory Park must be his! He wanted the old woman to repeat her story to Lord Shelford but she refused. She still believed that if the Felk family found out about Jed, he would be killed."

"So when Martha refused, what did Jed plan to do then?" asked Charles.

"He said he would claim his birthright – another way," answered Esmé. "*He* must marry Davina and not Howard. He wanted me to go to Davina and tell her about – Howard and me. Then she would abandon the wedding.

"I told Jed that first I must find out if Howard loved Davina. If he did not love her, I would do as Jed asked. But if I discovered that he *did* love her, then I would not destroy his happiness. I would say nothing, but I would kill myself!"

Both Davina and Charles exclaimed in horror, but Howard chuckled with pride.

"By God, she's a passionate creature!" he said. "I had no idea all this was going on, of course, until later that same day, when I encountered Jed in the woods. He said nothing about what he had discovered from the old woman, but he couldn't contain himself about Esmé.

"When he said she was living in the woods, it put the wind up me, I can tell you. And when he started ranting that I must honour my commitment to her, I said he should mind his own business. Next he had me off my horse and was using his fists on me. Damned unpleasant it was, too. It didn't help that Davina stumbled on to us – "

Charles started. "Davina?"

"Yes," continued Howard. "She didn't know what the fight was about, of course, and I immediately sent her back

161

to the house. Jed threw a few more punches but I managed to get away.

"I couldn't get Esmé out of my mind, though. I wanted to see her just – one more time. So that evening after supper, I slipped away. I started out for the woods. But it seems Esmé had the same idea, for there she was, riding towards me.

"I knew the minute I saw her again, what I felt for her. We embraced and I was even more certain. Then the house went up in flames and without thinking we raced back. When I saw her risk her life I thought, '*Howard, old fellow, she's the one for you after all.*'"

Howard gave a sheepish grin. "I really didn't mean to put noses out of joint, you know!"

Charles shook his head. "I simply cannot imagine what Esmé could ever want with a shallow fool like you!"

Esmé sprang up with a cry. "I love him. Yes, weakling and coward though he is, I love him. Why is it a surprise that I should love him? After all, Davina loves him too."

Davina's head swam in sudden shock. *Love Howard*? When had she given Esmé that impression? She glanced at Charles. His face was impassive, but his knuckles where he gripped the sword had tightened.

"Oh?" he said dryly. "That is no concern of mine."

Esmé regarded him strangely and then shrugged. "If you say so. But she came to this very cottage to seek me out. I supposed she wanted to see what kind of – rival she had. She admitted she loved Howard. I remember her words exactly. '*You know nothing of me. Only that I am to marry and that I love the man you love!*'"

Davina gasped as she realised how Esmé had concluded from that remark that the man Davina was to marry – Howard – was one and the same as the man she loved!

Davina stole a glance at Charles. His face was set as if in stone. The only movement was the flexing of a muscle in his jaw.

Howard plucked at his chin anxiously. "I never realised that Davina cared much for me at all, Charles. Truly I didn't. Esmé, on the other hand, had always made her feelings clear."

He fell silent as his brother turned a coldly enquiring gaze upon him.

"Perhaps you would like to make clear, sir, just what your intentions now are regarding Esmé!"

"Oh – to marry her, Charles. To marry her."

He tapped the sword against his boot. "Are you not forgetting something? You are not *free* to marry, sir. You are already betrothed."

Davina's mind reeled. Did Charles intend to try and force Howard to marry her, Davina, so that he might once again pursue Esmé? Nothing could be more cruel or devastating!

She staggered to her feet, tears filling her eyes. "He *is* free, Lord Delverton, because I release him. I release him from his promise. Esmé – he is yours."

Gathering the cloak about her, she turned for the door. When Charles put out a hand to bar her way, she swung angrily upon him.

"I am leaving. I am taking your horse and if you try to prevent me I – will kill you!"

She rushed furiously out into the rain. All she could hear behind her was Esmé's admiring laughter.

"Bravo, little Davina," she called. "Bravo!"

*

The sun was setting over the lake, casting a pale golden glow on the water. Davina, wrapped in a plaid blanket and a fur, stared over the tranquil scene from the terrace of Priory Park.

She had been ill for some weeks after her mad gallop home from the cottage in the woods. Regine had nursed her but this morning had finally departed for London with the Duke of Bedley and Mrs. Crouch.

Meanwhile Jess had relayed all news of what had ensued after that fateful afternoon at the cottage in the woods.

Howard and Esmé had gone to Liverpool. There they had married before setting sail for a new life in America.

Charles's horse, that Davina had ridden so hard and fast, had been returned to its master after a spell of cosseting in the Priory Park stables. Both Charles and Aunt Sarah had visited on a number of occasions to enquire after Davina's health but Davina had been too ill to see anyone.

Now she had recovered she made it clear to her father that she wished to return to London. That way, she thought to herself, she would never have to see Charles again.

Footsteps sounded on the stones of the terrace. She opened her eyes and then started to her feet in shock.

"L-Lord Delverton!"

It was as if her thoughts had conjured up his image! Horrified, she gathered up her fur, with the full intention of fleeing into the house.

"Madam, I beg you. Give me leave to speak to you, please."

His voice was so low and so full of pleading, that Davina hesitated and then sank back slowly into her chair. Charles watched her for a moment before stooping to lift the edge of her fur from where it trailed on the ground.

She took it from him without a word and waited.

"Since we – were last together," said Lord Delverton eventually, "my circumstances have unexpectedly changed for the better. The letter you delivered to me that afternoon in the cottage – was from Africa. It brought news that diamonds had at last been discovered in my mine. I am now, it appears, a very rich man indeed."

He paused as if to gauge Davina's response.

"I am delighted – at your good fortune," she said mechanically.

Charles regarded her closely and sighed. "I had hoped you would understand what this sudden access of wealth actually means to me," he said softly.

Davina considered, plucking at the edges of the fur. "Well, I suppose it means you can buy foreign cheeses and the best sherry and feather beds and – and lots of Wedgewood china."

His lips twitched. "That is all correct, of course. But it also means that, at long last, I have something concrete to offer a – a wife."

"No doubt that is an advantageous development for you," she murmured, wondering what this information had to do with her.

"For pity's sake, madam," Charles exclaimed. "Can you not see that I am asking for your hand in marriage?"

Davina froze. *He pitied her*! She had been abandoned by his brother and he pitied her! Why else would he ask her to marry him, when his own heart yearned for Esmé?

"I could not possibly consider such an offer," she replied icily. She turned her head and stared out over the darkening lake.

Such a long silence ensued that at last she thought he might have departed. She turned back to see him standing there still, his head low, his eyes fixed on the ground.

"Madam," he said, and she was surprised at the tremor in his voice. "I do understand – that it will take time for you to – to forget my brother."

Davina could not help her reply. "As long as it will take you to – to forget the gypsy, perhaps?"

Charles reeled. "Esmé? You cannot believe I was enamoured of *Esmé*? She is an extraordinary creature and worth ten of my brother but – I was never free to love her."

Davina's heart gave a curious flutter in her breast. "N-never free?"

"No, for from the moment I saw you, my heart was in your hands. Alas, fate so conspired that, before I had the courage to divulge my feelings, you were engaged to Howard. Then oh, how I tried to tear you from my soul but – it was impossible. How bitter it was to me that you loved him and – loathed me."

Wondering, suffused with an impossible hope, Davina rose trembling from her chair.

"You cannot know – " she began.

"Oh, madam," her companion groaned. "Do you think I cannot know how deep a wound may be inflicted by the arrow of love? Yet allow me to hope that I might heal that wound in you!"

Davina gazed in awe at his tortured features. Could all that he was saying be true?

"At the time of the fire," she whispered, "when I fell – from the rope – was it you who caught me?"

"Yes, it was."

She began to tremble, remembering the passionate words that had poured forth as she lay dazed in his arms.

"*Thank God. Thank God, my darling. You are safe.*"

Charles, trying to control the emotion in his voice, now ventured his own question.

"The brooch – that I took from you on the terrace – when you returned in so distraught a state from the woods – did you accept it willingly from Jed?"

166

Davina shuddered. "No, oh, no! He pressed the brooch – and his most unwelcome attentions – on me. I fled his touch."

There was a sharp intake of breath. "He – laid hands on you?"

Davina buried her face in her hands. "Yes," she admitted in a trembling voice.

Charles clenched his fist. "By God, he is lucky to be dead and beyond my reach."

Davina looked up breathlessly into his burning eyes.

His features, taut with fury at the insolence of Jed, melted as he looked at her. Yet still he misinterpreted her gaze.

"How you have suffered," he said, quivering with emotion. "My only hope is that you will permit time and my devoted attention to erase from your mind the memory of both Jed Barker and my charming but dishonourable brother, Howard."

At the word 'dishonourable,' Davina, dazed beyond all measure by the turn of events, burst into tears.

"He said – he said – you dallied with many ladies and – squandered your family's fortune on them!"

"*Howard* said that?"

Davina nodded miserably. At last, Charles understood. Seeing her tear-streaked face turned to him, he reached out his hand and hesitantly but tenderly pushed back a strand of golden hair from her brow.

"Did he – tell you that while – offering endearments to you?" he asked gently.

"Y-yes," whispered Davina.

"Oh, my darling girl, can you not see that he was securing you for himself by painting an unsavoury picture of me? I have only ever dreamed of happiness with one woman on earth and that is *you*!"

Convinced at last that Charles did indeed love her, Davina cried out, "And I, my Lord – have dreamed only of you! But once betrothed to Howard, how could I ever admit my deep love for you?"

His eyes alight, Charles sank to one knee.

"Prove that you dreamed of me, my darling! Take my hand now and promise that you will be mine forever. Marry me, my adored one, marry me!"

The touch of his hand made Davina swoon. She would have fallen, but with one swift move, he was on his feet again and folding her within his arms.

She would surely die in his embrace, die as she felt his strong arms encircle her waist! Then came his whispering breath on her cheek.

"Your answer, my sweetheart? Your answer?"

"Y-yes, my Lord. Yes!"

He moaned as he bent to kiss her.

She felt his lips seeking hers and his was the sweetest kiss she could ever have imagined. A kiss that would enchant her for the rest of their lives together. A kiss that would become a symbol of their devotion to each other.

The joy that swept through her whole being brought such an incredible sensation of happiness that no words could express her feelings now or forever.

She found herself suddenly in a new universe of delight so distant from the world of all the misery and drama of recent events.

Her heart pounding, Davina strained her breast to his. Now at last the struggle was over. Now at last they might be one.

Now at last they could claim the love that was *theirs to eternity*.